A Dangerous
HOMECOMING

SUSAN YAWN TANNER

Also by Susan Yawn Tanner

The Bellamys of Texas historical series:
Winds Across Texas
Fire Across Texas
Storm Out of Texas

The Bellamy Legacy contemporary series:
A Dangerous Inheritance
A Dangerous Charade
A Dangerous Homecoming

New editions from Secret Staircase Books
The Scottish Highlands Romances
Highland Captive
Captive to a Dream
Exiled Heart

A Warm Southern Christmas
(a historical romance novella)

The Cat Callahan Mysteries
Callahan and the Horses of Hope
Callahan Goes Rodeo
Callahan in Action
A Callahan Christmas (short story)

A Dangerous HOMECOMING

The Bellamy Legacy
Book 3

SUSAN YAWN TANNER

Secret Staircase Books

A Dangerous Homecoming
Published by Secret Staircase Books, an imprint of
Columbine Publishing Group LLC
PO Box 416, Angel Fire, NM 87710

Book layout and design by Secret Staircase Books
First trade paperback edition: September, 2025
First e-book edition: September, 2025

Publisher's Cataloging-in-Publication Data

Tanner, Susan Yawn
A Dangerous Homecoming / by Susan Yawn Tanner.
p. cm.
ISBN 978-1649142276 (paperback)
ISBN 978-1649142283 (e-book)

1. Jonah Slade (Fictitious character)—Fiction. 2. New Mexico—
Fiction. 3. Private Investigators—Fiction. 4. Western Contemporary
Romantic Suspense—Fiction. I. Title

The Bellamy Legacy Series : Book 3.
Tanner, Susan Yawn, Bellamy Legacy romantic suspense.

BISAC : FICTION / Romantic Suspense.

813/.54

*For Zoey and Kila, my beautiful granddaughters,
because blood is not the only tie that binds.*

Acknowledgements

If imagination is the soul of storytelling, then readers—especially beta readers—are surely the heart of it, and I'm grateful for mine. A special thanks to my beta readers: Susan Gross, Sandra Anderson, Eve Osborne, Dawn Hasiotis, Amy Connolley, Paula Webb, Isobel Tamney, Donna Townsend, and Georgia Ryle.

Prologue

A single gull floated in an arc above the oil rig. Glenn Collier followed it with his eyes, even as his brain remained engaged with the mechanical issues his team was working to resolve. Production was king, and a delay in drilling wasn't acceptable on any level. Even with that, safety came first with him, and every person on the rig knew it.

His safety engineer hovered, which was why Glenn kept his back to the activity behind him and his attention focused on the leaden sky and the silvery currents that rippled as far as the eye could see. Watching their every move would only make them tense, less productive and more inclined to make a mistake that could get one of them hurt. His role was to support and appreciate the expertise of his crew. He had some of the best in the business, and their paychecks reflected his belief in them.

Less than half an hour later, a soft cheer mingled with a few muttered curses of relief, and he turned with a smile for his team. The engine rumbled to life before settling into a steady throb. The foreman took a step back and gave Glenn a grin and a thumbs up as the crew began to reassemble the casing. Glenn returned the grin with a nod of appreciation. Further appreciation would be coming to the entire team in the form of an additional month's pay. But that would be his long-distance surprise. It was past time for him to be back in his office.

Another problem waited for him there, a bigger problem, but he was damned if he knew exactly what it was. At least now he could focus on it, if only long enough to put it aside as a non-issue, as he hoped would be the case.

He watched as his recently-promoted pilot walked toward him. "Your aircraft is ready, sir."

"Thanks, Keira. I'll grab my bags … and I told you to drop the sir."

"Bags already loaded. Sir." She gave him a cheeky grin, and he rolled his eyes. "What, you're going to get rid of me like you did the last guy?"

Since the last guy now owned a helicopter charter service, compliments of Glenn's financial backing, he didn't bother to answer.

Chapter One

Jade Bellamy slipped her heels off under her desk and stretched her toes and the arches of her feet. It had been a meeting kind of day. Not her favorite. That in itself didn't dictate heels, but these meetings had been a series of discussions with state officials, some of whom were decidedly unhappy with their city counterparts for utilizing the services of the Slade Agency which, along with the Bellamy Ranch, was under the umbrella of Welles Enterprises. It was all posturing, in her opinion, a means of jockeying for pole position in the state's political arena. Jade wasn't overly short, but nor was she overly tall; the heels were simply a hint of her own power play. As her Uncle Reggie would say, 'anything to level the playing field', at which he was a pro. And so was she.

She was also very good at explaining what the Slade Agency brought to the table in any investigation. Not only did she believe it, she lived it. But none of that seemed to matter in a room filled with testosterone. The only thing that had soothed the troubled waters was her blunt reminder that the Slade Agency always delivered, and neither the state nor the city was ever charged for any assistance provided.

With a sigh, she reached for the small stack of unopened mail her assistant had left for her. The first few were easily dispensed with, two more required some thought and assignments to gather further information. She scribbled a different team member's name on each. Her hand stilled above the next. The handwriting was distinctive in its precision, no return address.

With a faint frown, she slid the letter opener through the back of the envelope. The paper was precisely cut to fit the legal-sized envelope with a single line of hand-printed text centering it. "I know where the body is buried."

She pulled open a narrow desk drawer and withdrew another envelope. Sliding the single precisely cut paper from within, she compared the handwriting. Identical. As she'd known they would be, but who or why or what remained a mystery. The postmarks were both local, and exactly one week apart. She read the single line from the first note again. "I know who died."

Her brow furrowed. The words made no more sense now than they had a week ago. The single line hadn't seemed a threat, exactly, nor a warning. The word was *died*, not *murdered* or *killed*. But with the addition of the second note, the implications were there. The reference to a buried body implied an illicit act, something unlawful or even sinister. The fact that the first note and the second one had been addressed to her personally held at least a hint of menace. Still, at this point, there was little she could do. She didn't know who had died or when, much less where or why … and more importantly, how. All she could do was wait.

Whatever the game, she wouldn't go chasing after phantoms. Patience might not be her strong suit, but neither was anxiety her weakness. She placed both notes back in their respective envelopes, then pushed them and her curiosity into her briefcase.

A light rap drew her attention to the door she'd left open. She kept her expression pleasant as she let her glance sweep the man who had propped one shoulder against the doorframe in a pose probably intended to be suave. "You ran away."

Jade lifted a brow, wondering why blonde hair and dimples had never appealed to her quite as much as dark eyes and a rugged jaw. Life could have been so much simpler. "I haven't run from or toward anything since the last home run I hit in college." While that wasn't quite true, it was a good line, or so she told herself.

"I'd planned to invite you to lunch. Is it too late?"

"Business or pleasure?" she countered.

"Hopefully a bit of both."

Her gaze held steady on his, and he sighed. "Fine. Business … and confidential."

She pushed her heels further aside and slipped her feet into the comfortable flats she'd abandoned earlier.

He waited as she got to her feet and walked toward him before adding with a hint of frustration, "But that doesn't mean I won't enjoy spending time with you."

She chuckled. "You enjoy women, Leo, all women." Her sidelong glance held curiosity. "And business is always confidential with me. You know that."

"I do." He stepped aside to let her pass, then placed one hand lightly at her waist.

Jade left it. Although she was perfectly capable of causing a scene at any time and any place, she suspected there was something to this business the city attorney wanted to discuss. Something bothersome. If she elbowed him for that misplaced hand, she might never learn what it was.

He frowned when they entered the elevator and she pressed the button beside the word restaurant. "I made reservations elsewhere."

"Cancel them. I've got a busy afternoon, and 'wining and dining' isn't on my schedule."

"You make your own schedule, and you know it," he grumbled.

"Which is why I know what is and isn't on it."

The hostess greeted them at the door and led them toward the booth Jade favored for business discussions. With several others, it formed a semi-circle around the hostess station. The drawback was no view of the windows or the sidewalk scene beyond. The benefit was quiet and privacy … a sense of solitude … and a soundproofing design that kept quietly spoken secrets contained.

Jade waited until their waiter brought them glasses of water and took their orders before leaning back and meeting Leo's gaze. "So, talk."

"The Director of City Council Services is being blackmailed."

She hid the fact that her heart jumped slightly, that he'd caught her off-guard. She couldn't help but think of the envelopes in her briefcase. "Paul Cargill?"

Leo nodded.

"By whom?"

That drew a shrug.

"For what?"

Another shrug.

Jade shook her head. "He won't tell you?"

"He can't. He doesn't know."

"I get that the blackmailer isn't willing to give a name, but Cargill must have some suspicion based on the point of blackmail."

"He doesn't know that either."

Jade shifted forward, placing her forearms on the table. "That isn't logical." No more logical for him than for her, but that point wasn't, and wouldn't be, up for discussion. "*Somebody* contacted him and said 'give me money or else I'll talk'? And Cargill is clueless about what that talk might reveal?"

"Pretty much." He fell silent as the waiter returned with their drinks.

She wasn't sure Leo believed what he'd been told. She wouldn't have bought it either, not before last week. But she held her tongue on both counts for the moment.

"You believe him?"

She waited for Leo to lie as he lifted his glass, tilting it as if fascinated by the chips of ice that danced on the surface, but he surprised her.

"Honestly, I'm not sure." He met her gaze. "I thought, at first, no, but he didn't seem afraid or angry. I'm a pretty damned good judge of character, Jade. All I got from our conversation was bewilderment and maybe a faint frustration over a waste of his time."

Jade shifted. That was damned close to her feelings about the notes she'd received. They had to be related, but the how, what, and why eluded her. And what if they weren't related? She considered the possibilities. Blackmail wasn't a rare occurrence. Not in the world of political wheeling and dealing.

Leo sighed and said what they both were thinking. "If he *doesn't* know what he's being blackmailed for, it could mean there's more than one possibility."

But that didn't fit for Jade. Cargill was sometimes bullheaded, often irascible, but dishonest didn't come anywhere close to her opinion of him.

"Or," she said finally, softly, "he thinks someone close to him could possibly be guilty of something or made to look guilty." But that someone didn't exist in her world. Or did it?

She took a breath. She had to focus on Cargill's situation. Maybe it merged with hers, *likely* it merged with hers, but maybe it didn't, and she'd figure out that aspect later.

Leo considered the suggestion. "He has a daughter in college and a son in grad school." He sighed. "Kids get themselves into all kinds of situations these days."

Jade nodded. "And his wife isn't in the picture anymore, last I heard." New boyfriend, new life.

"Even so, I think he'd protect her."

"From herself?" She lifted a brow.

"Likely." Leo shrugged. "Men are stupid that way."

Maybe so, she thought, but that shoe fit both sexes, and she said as much out loud.

"Regardless, Cargill wants you to take the case."

"I'll have Colter or Jonah give him a call."

"Not the Slade Agency," Leo said. "You."

"Me?" She stared at him stunned for a moment, then shook her head. "Leo, you know that's not what I do with the agency. And *I* know it's not what I'm best at." She found the investigative research tedious and much preferred moving the chess pieces around to make things happen.

"He trusts you."

The secret she'd kept all those years ago, the strings she'd pulled to keep his younger sister's name out of the headlines after a joyride with friends had gone wrong.

She tilted her head. "But not Colter and Jonah?"

"He doesn't distrust them."

She wanted to argue. Knowing damned well she didn't plan to bring her cousins into whatever was knocking at her own door kept that argument unspoken. Not that it was a lack of trust. She trusted Colter and Jonah with her life. When she knew more, she promised herself she'd bring them into the loop on whatever it was, whoever it was.

"How was he contacted?"

"Mail."

"That was risky. His secretary … any of his staff … could as easily have opened that envelope."

"Except the return address was his with his name above it." Leo hesitated, then added, "On both of them."

She stilled. "He's had two?"

"The second one came today. I think that's what convinced him to reach out to you."

Jade thought about that for a moment. "So, his address … as if he'd mailed something to himself for safekeeping? That would look suspicious."

Leo shrugged. "Regardless, it worked. No one touched them." He waited a few moments before asking, "Well?"

She leaned back as a server approached with their food. When they were alone again, he repeated his question, "Well?"

"I want the notes or letter or whatever."

He pulled a sealed legal-sized manila envelope from

his attaché case and passed it across the table. "I haven't actually seen the notes. Cargill had them taped up in this envelope when he handed it to me, but I can tell you he wasn't happy."

No one would be, Jade thought. She dropped the envelope into her briefcase. "I also want Cargill's fingerprints. If there are fingerprints that don't match his, we'll need those of anyone in his office who might have touched the notes." Since Leo hadn't, that was one less set of prints to muddy the water.

Leo winced, and Jade started eating. When he stayed silent, she gave him another look. "You know very well they're all on file."

"But the breach of confidentiality…"

"I wouldn't need names; labels would do. Person one, two, three or a, b, c. Hell, I don't care. If they're staff and had no reason to touch either note or envelope, you could decide what to do with that information. I'd only want to know which, if any, came from someone outside his office."

"And if none did?"

"The blackmailer is on staff or we're dealing with someone savvy enough to wear gloves."

He lifted a brow. "Which most people are these days, if only due to the recent popularity of police procedurals in novels and movies."

"True enough," she acknowledged.

"What else?"

Jade sighed. "I warned you I'm not the expert. That would be Colter and Jonah, remember? I had enough trouble coming up with that much." And that was God's own truth, but it would give her an opportunity to see if there was a match to any possible fingerprints on the notes she'd received and that was worth something. And if the notes she'd received and Cargill's were somehow connected, that was worth even more.

Leo stood when she did. "So, I'll tell Paul you'll be in touch?"

"In a day or two, yes. I'll have forensics look at the notes, then I'll want to meet with him, probably here, probably for breakfast."

Leo frowned unhappily. "He won't like it."

"I have questions. If he wants my help, he'll answer them." When Leo gazed pointedly around at the other diners and raised his brow, she shrugged. "A casual encounter with a 'how's the family' conversation will get less notice than if we meet in either of our offices. If he'd rather, you can come with him, then take a call and have to leave. Whatever works, but that meeting is non-negotiable. And, Leo, tell Cargill to pass me a piece of paper or something with his prints."

Leo nodded and she watched thoughtfully as he walked away. She didn't like quirks of fate. Didn't much believe in them as a rule. But they did happen from time to time, and the lack of similarity in the return address stood out. The notes to her had none. The notes to Cargill had his name as both sender and recipient. But if the wording of the messages proved identical, then there was no possibility of happenstance.

Possibly someone thought targeting two public figures would be a good power play or a confusing factor if brought to police attention. Apparently, Cargill had no more intention of doing that than she did. She knew her reasons for not doing so. She didn't know Cargill's.

Chapter Two

With one foot propped against a deck rail, Glenn watched the sun sink without hurry over the Gulf of Mexico. Florida was home, and home was right where he wanted to be. Given a choice, it was where he'd choose to stay, with its flat peninsula above him and white sandy beaches and open expanse of calm waters before him. Those slow, rolling waves were enticingly visible the entire length of his verandah.

Unfortunately, choices didn't always swing his way, and there was unexpected business to deal with. The past was nothing he wanted to revisit, but fate rarely gave a damn what humans wanted.

The first note had drawn a snort at someone's idea of a sick joke. "I know who died." The second, postmarked a week later, had changed the tone and changed his reaction.

"I know where the body is buried." That one held a definite menace, which pissed him off. The return addresses on both were the same. Blank. But the postmarks on both were Albuquerque. He knew he hadn't left any friends in New Mexico, but whoever was playing games could go to hell.

He turned his attention from the purpling sky to the envelopes on the side table next to him. He'd have to deal with them at some point. *How* wasn't clear yet. They'd both been waiting for his return from the oil rig, which had taken longer than expected. That wasn't anything he minded except for the loss of revenue while repairs were made. Being with his various crews on the rigs scattered throughout the gulf was—to him—time better spent than in any meeting or conference call.

As if on cue, a muted tone drew his attention to the phone he'd dropped carelessly onto the wide-plank floor beside him. He couldn't see the caller and considered ignoring the insistent sound, then sighed as he scooped it up.

"Glenn … hi." Lizbeth's husky voice was a visceral tug on his senses, as was always the case.

"Hi, yourself." He settled in for a lazy chat and a few minutes of wishing theirs wasn't a mostly long distant relationship. "How was London?"

"Dismal. City streets and rain." She yawned, and he could almost see her sleek, catlike stretch. "How are the Keys?"

"Lazy."

"Perfect. I can be there by the weekend. And, Glenn … I'm thinking this would all be easier if we were married. I miss you when we're thousands of miles apart."

Lately, Glenn had been thinking the same. He and

Lizbeth were compatible in every way. In the months after their first dinner date, she'd gradually edged out pleasant evenings with high-profile women, filling an emptiness he hadn't realized existed in spite of his career successes and that string of women.

Then the first note had come, reminding him of old baggage left behind. He hadn't changed his mind, but that old business might have to be settled first, and now, it appeared, additional complications might have to be unraveled.

Even with that hanging over him, he and Lizbeth had a good thing going, maybe not the sweet heat he'd once known and been too damned young to savor but surely enough physical and emotional compatibility to make a solid marriage. "How about we meet in New Orleans Friday? Maybe take a stroll through some jewelry shops and find a ring that puts a smile on your face."

"You already do that, Glenn, with or without a ring. All it takes is the thought of you. I'm smiling now."

He smiled, too. "I'll make reservations for our favorite suite and restaurants for the weekend."

And then he'd deal with whatever waited in New Mexico and finish what should never have been started, but … hell … if eighteen wasn't the time to make dumb mistakes, when was?

Beyond that were the two letters that were beginning to feel like a lead-in to blackmail. For what, he hadn't a clue, but he was damned sure it had something to do with the Bellamys. They'd hated him, as it turned out, and he hadn't thought much of them in the end. Regardless, he'd finish all of that, too, at least as far as his involvement was concerned.

* * *

Glenn walked into the boardroom five minutes before nine the next morning and was pleased to see everyone seated and comfortable, with coffee and food in front of them.

He took his place at the far end of the table and gave a nod to his CEO at the other. His team knew him well. Information was concise and delivered without fanfare. Business remained good, despite the swinging pendulum of politics. Neither major party wanted to interfere too drastically in the oil business when the electric grid was already taking a beating over coal-fired units, most of which had recently been retired. That would change eventually. Collier Oil would be ready when it did.

The last to address the group was his attorney.

Glenn couldn't read her face. He never could. "What do you have for us, Ellie?"

She signaled to her assistant, who passed folders around the table, one for each of his board members, then carried the last one over to Glenn.

Still watching Ellie, Glenn finally caught a glint of satisfaction. Good news then.

She took a deep breath. "Our exploration and findings were approved. The temporary oil lease for Collier 24 has expired and a production lease awarded based on findings submitted."

Glenn felt a surge of satisfaction, as much for the team in front of him as for himself. "Well done, Ellie."

Everyone in the room knew this was a serious victory. Offshore oil and gas lease sales would be severely curtailed now that the current administration's lease plan was firmly in place. His team barely had this last temporary exploration lease secured before the new restrictions were signed into law. If that exploration had proven in vain, there wouldn't have been another opportunity.

Collier Oil differed from most oil companies in that its oil rigs were owned by a subsidiary company rather than leased from an independent. At times it was a headache, but it also offered some security going forward.

He looked around the room. "My thanks to each one of you. A tremendous amount of work—successful work—went into number 24. You can all be proud, and you'll share in the rewards from your combined effort."

At the close of the meeting, no one was in a hurry to leave. Glenn allowed them their time for self-congratulations on all of the intense nights and reports and scrutiny that had brought them here. But, as they began to wander out, Glenn asked Ellie to stay behind. She finished her conversation with one of her interns and returned to the table, but didn't sit. He could tell she expected this to be brief. His conversations usually were. Succinct and to the point.

At Glenn's request, his assistant closed the conference room door on his way out, and Ellie lifted her brow. A closed door with Glenn indicated a not-so-typical conversation.

Ellie propped a hip against the table. Her Haitian blood gave her an exotic look. Dark eyes reflected sharp intelligence, which Glenn knew to be far above average, and a steely determination to succeed. He valued those characteristics, but it was her loyalty and discretion he valued most.

She tilted her head in query. "What's up, boss?"

Glenn sighed. "I need you to confirm whether or not I'm still married to Jade Bellamy-Davidson."

Ellie pulled her chair out and sat. "Well … hell. I didn't

expect that."

"No," Glenn said ruefully. "I don't suppose you did."

"Of *the* Bellamys?"

"Afraid so."

"How long ago was this?"

"Sixteen years in September."

She blinked. "You were … what? Eighteen?"

"But legal." It sounded crazy to him now, but damned sure hadn't felt it at the time.

"Barely. And Jade?"

"Same. Believe me, we were well and truly married." He pulled his briefcase closer and withdrew an envelope. "A copy of the marriage certificate, duly signed and executed."

She unfolded it slowly, read it through, then gave him a pained look. "All these years, building a life—hell, an empire—and you did nothing to protect yourself? Is New Mexico a community property state?"

He shrugged. "I've no idea. You're the attorney."

She blew out a breath. "So, yeah, I'll find out. The sooner, the better. Anything else I need to know? Kids, for example?"

"None." At least as far as he knew, and he had checked as best he could. It had taken him a year to find a job steady enough to get him on his feet, but, yeah, he'd checked. That assurance had been one of his first major purchases, long before a home, long before a vehicle. He would never have left a child of his at the mercy of Jade's family. For years, he'd been haunted by the possibility that she had been with child and terminated the pregnancy. He'd had to put those thoughts aside for his own sanity.

Ellie got to her feet and crossed the room but turned back at the door. "I'm guessing this decision *now* has to do with Lizbeth."

Glenn smiled faintly. They were friends enough, long enough, she could ask that question, knowing he wouldn't mind. And he didn't. "She thinks it's time."

"And what do you think?"

"We're compatible." Lizbeth, at least, wouldn't have her family, or their hired hands, beat the shit out of him and dump him over the state line if she decided their marriage was a mistake. Lizbeth—her kind—were civilized. There was damned little civility in any Bellamy that he'd ever met.

Ellie opened the door and gave him a steady look. "We'll talk more later. I'll let you know what I find out."

It occurred to Glenn she'd probably do some digging into Lizbeth's financials as well, which was fine. He knew they'd hold up. He doubted Ellie would be in a hurry, but, hell, he wasn't either. Still, like Lizbeth, he supposed it was time.

Jade's family had a shitload to answer for, but he'd let someone else make that happen, and, eventually, it would. All he wanted was out. Out of the past, out of the memories, out of the Bellamy snares. It was time to move on.

Chapter Three

Jade left her dinner half-eaten and carried her glass to the spare room she'd converted into an office. She cleared her desk, systematically putting some things away and trashing others, before pulling on a pair of clear plastic gloves she'd bought after leaving the office for the day. Taking Cargill's envelope from her briefcase, she slit the tape. Her stomach tensed as she withdrew the notes and placed them side by side with the ones she'd been sent, hers on the left, Cargill's on the right. All had been precision cut to fit the envelopes, and the wording on both sets was identical. She was no hand-writing expert, but she wasn't half bad, and that appeared identical as well.

She leaned back with a frown. She and Cargill had absolutely nothing in common except geography and that long ago favor. They interacted on a professional level, certainly, but those times were few and far between and had never been an occasion for drama of any kind, much less a reason for blackmail, particularly one involving a death.

Her instinct was still to bring Jonah and Colter in on this, and that remained a strong option and a stronger possibility. Because the director was part of the mix, it all felt less personal, and therefore, somehow, less threatening. But, to assuage Cargill and give herself time to think, she'd do some research first into his business associates prior to his position with the city. While his work was important, it was rarely newsworthy or flamboyant. He didn't often interact with the true movers and shakers of the area. He kept the council on task and, from all she knew, he was well-liked and thought to be an effective administrator. If he'd ever stirred the pot with anyone, she couldn't recall the occasion.

Prior to his current role, he'd been a corporate attorney for one of the larger trucking companies in the state. She couldn't recall any major conflicts or scandals, but that didn't mean there weren't any. What they might have in common with her was the sticking point. She was much more likely to have some connection with city business than anything to do with the trucking industry. But it seemed unlikely that there would be anything that linked her and Cargill.

Feeling the tension tightening her shoulders, she stood and stretched. Nothing she really needed to do could be done before morning. A half an hour on her elliptical would work the kinks from her muscles. She laughed at herself as she picked up the wine she had yet to touch, but as she reached for the light switch, the laughter faded. Turning back to her desk, she did something she'd never felt the need to do … not in her own apartment. She placed all four notes back in their envelopes, put them in her center desk drawer, then locked it.

Maybe a hot shower instead, she thought, and finish that wine. The elliptical could wait until morning.

But, by morning, even before she'd had her first cup of coffee, much less had any thought of exercise, her brain had put a plan in place.

Before noon, she'd pulled financials on Cargill and family. The son was studying economics at Rice—funded by his proud paternal grandfather—and already lobbying for a government position which he'd likely get based on grades and civic involvement. His daughter was in her first year at the University of New Mexico with a course of basics, average grades, and a challenging evening class lending itself to a business degree. Interestingly, she was acing that evening class. She had an apartment in Albuquerque she shared physically and financially with a boyfriend as average as she was.

The ex-wife was the more interesting with a very flamboyant reputation for giving to the arts, apparently funded by the wealthy boyfriend. Her lump sum alimony from Cargill wasn't stingy but neither was it over the top. If she were smart, some of that lump sum was in savings and some of it was invested in stable markets. Jade wasn't betting on smart. Still, nothing there to suggest she was capable of any kind of blackmail scheme, much less one complicated enough to involve two potential victims and one of those a Bellamy. Nor did Jade see a need, despite her flashy lifestyle.

Few people in this part of the country intentionally took on a Bellamy. One newscaster had recently likened it to poking a stick into a den of bears. If you woke one, you woke them all. Which was true.

She was contemplating the notes she'd gathered when her assistant—tall, thin, and toned—rapped on her open door. Jade looked up with a smile that broadened as she saw the tray from the restaurant downstairs.

"Lori, you're a saint."

The young woman had the build of a kickboxer but always dressed far more professionally than Jade ever had unless going to a damnable meeting. She was efficient and pleasant, and one day she'd be managing a department. Jade had little doubt of that. And Jade would be sure to aid in that promotion when the time came.

"Not quite," Lori gave her a wink, "but I am bucking for a raise."

"Depends. What kind of soup is that?"

"Taco … packing heat."

"How about a small bonus this month, raise at the end of the quarter?" For the soup and so many other things.

"Deal! Eat while it's hot."

As Lori turned to go, Jade said, "I'll be out of the office most of the early afternoon. Feel free to enjoy a long lunch, maybe some window shopping. I may need you late today."

"You know if I window shop, I'll buy."

"Taco soup bonus," Jade reminded, and they exchanged smiles before Lori pulled her door closed behind her. Lori's often-voiced thought was that even the most important person deserved to eat in peace, and she made that happen for Jade as often as she could.

The soup was good and the heat real, Jade decided as

she finished and stood to stuff her notes in her briefcase.

The tech in the lab downstairs was one of the newly promoted. Simon came across as a little overeager, Jade had thought when they'd been introduced, but she'd read his supervisor's reviews and agreed with Colter and Jonah. He knew his craft and appeared to be as technically skilled as his expert instructor.

He stood in front of a file cabinet, replacing folders that had been stacked on a tray. She rapped on the door frame to get his attention.

"Miss Jade! Come in." His gaze turned anxious behind wire-rimmed glasses. "No one's here but me. Shall I call Robert to come back up? He went down for coffee and then on to a quick meeting across the street."

"Not at all. I'm sure you can help me."

His gaze went to her briefcase, and he straightened his shoulders. "Of course. Won't you sit down?" He gestured to a small table in one corner. "I'll set these aside."

"No, please. Finish what you're doing. I'm not in a hurry."

His expression still uncertain, he gave a small nod then slid another folder into its place in a lower drawer.

Accustomed to working wherever and whenever, Jade sat and immediately flipped open her phone, making notes on an upcoming presentation to several incoming businesses. Jonah and Colter weren't thrilled with taking on security for additional outside clients, but the city had been wooing these particular entities, and Reggie and Marcus had brought their weight to bear in the city's favor. Since the family patriarchs rarely interfered with day-to-day business, Jonah and Colter had conceded.

The city was grateful, and Jade was even busier than usual.

"Miss Jade…?"

She looked up with an immediate smile. "Sorry. I got lost in what I was doing." His tray was empty. "Are you ready?"

"Yes, ma'am. Of course."

He took the chair opposite her as she opened her briefcase. She withdrew the first note Cargill had received along with the second she'd received, each encased in a clear protective sleeve.

"I'll need fingerprints developed from each. And I touched one before I realized what was being handed to me. At some point, I may need a handwriting comparison to city and state criminal databases for a potential match."

After glancing without touching, Simon left the table long enough to gather up some materials, then pulled on a pair of gloves. He gave her a quick look. "Both from the same person."

"That would be my guess," she agreed with a nod, "but only based on the wording and a visual of the handwriting."

Before withdrawing either piece of paper, he used a marker to label one sleeve A and the other B. He removed one, made a copy, then switched on his UV light equipment and began taking photographs of the now-visible prints.

Jade stared at the orange glow. She was always fascinated by the process even though she had no desire to develop that expertise for herself. He replaced the first note in its sleeve and repeated the process with the other.

She stayed silent, watching him work. When he finished, he leaned back. "All I can tell you at this point is that there's one clear print on each note … but they aren't the same. Nor does the pattern seem to indicate they are prints from different fingers of the same person."

Hers, she thought, and Cargill's most likely. So, the

blackmailer wasn't stupid. But then, she hadn't thought he, or she, would be.

"Thanks, Simon. I appreciate that. I requested prints from the recipient, and I'll get those to you. Because I touched one before I realized what was being handed to me, you'll need to match to my prints on file with the company. I'll need a handwriting comparison to city and state criminal databases for a potential match. If there is an outlier from the fingerprints, I'll want that matched as well."

He put his equipment away and turned back to her. "Shall I turn this case over to Robert when he gets back?"

Jade shook her head. "This isn't a case … it's a favor for a friend. I'll keep the notes with me, and you can send me a set of the fingerprint and handwriting search results when that's done."

"The handwriting match would be more precise if done with originals," he reminded her.

"Only in regard to certain measurements," she agreed. "If we don't get what we need from the copies, I'll re-evaluate and make a recommendation to the owner."

"But you'll discuss this with Mr. Jonah and Mr. Colter?" He looked anxious.

Damn. Anxious and persistent. "No, actually, I won't. I was asked for only this much," she said firmly. "My friend will have to decide what to do next. This is as involved as the Slade Agency will be unless we're asked to do more. I plan to encourage my friend to turn it over to us officially or go to the police and let them handle it."

"Yes, ma'am. Hopefully she will. This could be a very dangerous situation."

Jade managed to not roll her eyes. How classic that the young tech assumed the friend was a woman in need.

Settled in her office, Jade had plenty to keep her busy while she waited to hear from Simon. As sure as she felt that the two notes were written by the same person, she wanted to rule out known criminals, especially blackmailers, before she spent hours combing through each person she and Cargill had in common. That would take a while, and she wasn't one to waste time needlessly.

She worked in peace until mid-afternoon when Colter rapped lightly at her open door. One look at his face had her leaning back in her chair with a sigh. Just what she'd been afraid of …

"Have a seat," she said dryly after he settled himself opposite her.

He shot her a grin at the hint of sarcasm, but it didn't reach his eyes. They were as hard as his voice. "Who sent you a blackmail note?"

Careful, she cautioned herself. She'd never lied to him or to Jonah. She didn't plan to start now. At least not an outright lie. She'd catch hell from him later, when all the facts were out, but she'd dealt with hell before. It no longer frightened her. Her cousins for sure didn't.

"I suppose Simon spoke out of turn."

"Stopped me in the hall, but I'll be damned if I'll call it out of turn."

"Leo asked to speak to me after the meeting yesterday morning."

Colter closed his mouth and waited. He didn't look happy, by any means, but neither did he look set to explode as he had when he walked in.

Jade stood and walked around her desk to close the door Colter had left open.

"Who does he think is blackmailing him?"

She sat, still choosing her words carefully. "Not him.

Cargill. Leo's the messenger boy."

"And Leo brought it to you?"

"He did, and I reminded him it wasn't my expertise. I wanted to hand it off to the agency."

"But?"

"Cargill's set on me."

Colter frowned. "Any particular reason?"

"Yes, but not one I can disclose. Something that happened a very long time ago. I saved his political ass, more by chance than plan, but he trusts me because of it." Her goal had been to prevent the ruin of a young girl's life from a dumb mistake. The fact that Cargill had benefited from the silencing of the media hadn't mattered nearly as much.

Colter seemed to contemplate that for a moment, then gave a short nod of acceptance. They both knew that kind of thing happened. "What have you got so far?"

The tension in her shoulders eased somewhat. "Little to nothing," she admitted as she pulled the notes from her briefcase, still in their plastic sleeves, and passed them to him.

He studied them for several minutes. "Not much to go on."

"As I said …" She hesitated. "I can't turn this over to you or even bring you in officially, but I wouldn't mind running things by you."

"Any time. You know that."

"Know it and appreciate it."

It was his turn to hesitate. "I know you can take care of yourself as well as anyone, Jade, but be careful. This could turn into something ugly."

"I'll watch my back."

"And let me know if you sense anything off."

"Like?"

"Anything sketchy."

"Blackmail's pretty damned sketchy," she countered. "If that's what it proves to be. Nothing's been asked yet."

His frustration showed. "Beyond that possibility. Like, maybe, Cargill not being honest with you. Or holding something back. You're good at what you do, but what you do doesn't usually involve your finger on a trigger."

But they knew that sometimes it did. She thought it, but didn't say it.

"My first plan of action is to talk with Cargill, whether he likes it or not. Beyond that, I'm current on training and practice." Her response wasn't defensive. She knew his words were absolute truth and came from the heart. "I'll watch my back and I'll let you know if things get out of kilter in any direction."

"I guess that will have to do."

She grinned at Colter's tone. "I guess it will." Her smile faded. Time, she thought, to change the subject and not only to take the heat off herself. "I saw we've had another missing person report."

Because of the pro bono work they frequently did for the chief of police, the Slade Agency was sent a daily briefing. Always confidential. In case the need arose.

"APD isn't calling either a kidnapping."

"Yet."

"There are similarities, but we're not being called in."

"Yet," she said again.

He nodded in agreement as he got to his feet. "I'm headed home. Let me know what you get from forensics on the fingerprints and handwriting."

"Probably nothing concrete," she admitted, "but I'll let

you know as soon as I have it. Give my best to Miranda and the boys."

Colter stopped at the door and gave her a long look of affection mixed with concern. "Always." Almost as an afterthought, he asked, "What are you going to do about your problem child?"

"Simon?" She shook her head. "I'm not sure yet. Besides, technically this is as much your problem as mine."

"No." Just the one word with a chuckle at her expression.

Even knowing he was right, didn't quell her irritation. "Yeah, I know. It's my case … unofficial as it is." Her case, her risk, and *this* was why she didn't want direct reports of her own, at least not beyond Lori who was a jewel. Performance management was a pain in the ass. "I'm not sure yet, but I'll deal with it."

His footsteps faded down the hall and she reached for her desk phone. "Lori, see if Robert has time to come to my office."

Chapter Four

Lizbeth tugged at his hand as they neared another jeweler's shop. "Not that one."

Glenn turned to look at her. Her blonde hair, more platinum than gold, gleamed in the sunlight. So far, the morning had been as much fun as he could make it for her. This would be their third stop. In the first, she'd bought him a watch he didn't need because it had caught her eye. In the second, a pair of cufflinks he would rarely have occasion to wear, but she was enchanted with the tiny, intricate carvings. He was beginning to feel like a kept man, and he'd told her so, at which she'd laughed with delight as she warned, "I plan for you to spend twice as much on our rings."

But not, it seemed, at this particular establishment.

"What's wrong with them? Their jeweler has an excellent rating for quality. One of the best in New Orleans."

"But they also buy from people who find themselves forced to sell to survive."

He nodded and said nothing more as they walked past the expanse of windows displaying some of the more costly creations in the city. The famed Lizbet, as she was known in her world, had once been as far down on her luck as anyone could be, slowly pawning the numerous jewels her porn-star mother had left her in order to buy groceries and pay rent as she finished her senior year of high school and entered a community college.

She accepted the next place on Glenn's list. There they found an engagement ring that she loved and he liked.

"It is an original creation?" Lizbeth asked.

"Original and one of a kind," the sleekly dressed salesclerk assured her.

Lizbeth smiled at Glenn. "This one."

"The diamond is exquisite," the clerk agreed, then added smoothly, "The one to the left is almost the same cut but a bit larger to allow additional facets and brilliance."

"This one."

Glenn smiled and shrugged at the clerk as he bent his head low to Lizbeth's. "We could have the jeweler add a scattering of tiny emeralds or rubies around the base." He knew she loved the colorful stones far more than diamonds.

"It's perfect as it is."

He also knew how stubborn she could be. He looked at the woman who'd worn a patient and friendly smile throughout their exchange. "This one, then, and we'll look at wedding bands as well."

"Our jeweler created a matching band for this one. It will also remain one of a kind." She located it, then placed it on the counter beside the diamond.

Lizbeth nodded. "Perfect. Glenn's must match as well."

"Of course. One moment."

When she returned, she placed a second, wider band beside the first and turned to Lizbeth. "Your hands are very fine-boned. Your rings will likely need sizing."

"And engraved—my name in his and his name in mine."

"We'll take care of everything. It will be exactly as you want it to be."

Glenn's band ended up fitting perfectly. He smiled because, yes, their rings were almost exactly twice Lizbeth's impulsive purchases for him, which had made her far happier than receiving the gifts had made him. He wasn't impressed by jewels but, had she not been with him, the diamond on her ring would have been far larger. They left the store, with a very pleased salesclerk beaming as they linked arms.

Lizbeth smiled at him with her heart in her eyes as they walked out, and Glenn hoped his love for her was enough. He did truly love her. He wanted her to be happy. But it wasn't the love he'd felt once before. He suspected nothing ever could be, and maybe that was the way of life and to be expected. All he knew was that the ending of that first love had been a devastation he never wanted to experience again. With Lizbeth, he felt certain he'd never have to.

She was a steady candle, not a blaze that would turn into an inferno.

* * *

Glenn leaned back as the server deftly shifted their drinks from the tray he held to the tabletop between them.

They'd been seated in a corner on the verandah of the restaurant as Glenn had requested when he had made their reservation the evening before.

When the server asked if they were ready to order, Lizbeth lifted her shoulders with a smile, admitting, "I haven't even looked at the menu."

Neither had Glenn. After listening to the specials of the day and placing drink orders, they'd talked of everything from current news events to where they might get away for a few days after their wedding.

"Give us about fifteen minutes," Glenn suggested.

He waited until the server withdrew, then reached for Lizbeth's hand and said, "There's an old-fashioned piece of me that needs to do this right."

Lizbeth placed her hand in his and tilted her head with a mischievous smile that had earned her admirers around the globe.

"Will you be my wife, Lizbeth?"

She laughed lightly. "Of course."

With the sun shining in her hair and her feelings shining in her eyes, Glenn felt more at peace than he could ever remember. After a brief interruption as their waiter returned and they placed their orders, they talked of wedding venues, with him leaning toward the more traditional, surrounded by friends, and her leaning toward bare feet on an island beach where no one knew either of them.

He'd give her what she wanted, he thought, because none of the fuss mattered as much to him as it did to her. And because she made him feel content and peaceful.

He almost ignored his phone when it vibrated silently with a text message, but the waiter arrived with their meals so he took that moment of interruption to make sure all hell hadn't broken loose on one of the rigs.

The message was from Ellie. No divorce. No annulment.

Well, hell.

* * *

Glenn had never before had to pretend with Lizbeth, but today he did, first through lunch then through a lazy afternoon of drinks on the private balcony that opened from their upstairs room. Side by side in loungers, he savored a bourbon while she sipped margaritas poured into a ridiculously small glass from a pitcher on the table between them.

The hotel had once been an antebellum home; now it was a luxury inn in a secluded setting that also managed to be no more than a few minutes from the hustle and bustle of the city proper. They'd found it a year or so ago and had returned a time or two since. It was an easy choice in a city they both enjoyed.

In her lap was a room-service menu, flipped to the mostly blank back side. She'd grinned at him after writing 'wedding planner' at the top in her mostly unreadable scrawl. "So, small and private."

That was the first thing they'd agreed upon. Lizbeth loved the limelight but only when she was on the runway. And, at this stage in her career, those runways were all exclusive, private, and, therefore, expensive.

With her mother now out of the picture, her family was small but loving. He'd been sent away from his so many years ago that those ties had been broken. He'd seen them since, but they hadn't grown close. There were probably not a dozen guests on either of their lists.

"A small cake," she murmured, "with fancy hors d'oeuvres

and lots of them."

While Lizbeth made notes, his mind wrestled with the problem he hadn't known faced him. He tried not to think about it, not while he was with Lizbeth, and the truth was, while it impacted both of them, he had no intention of talking with her about it. Not until it was resolved which would be as damned fast as Ellie could arrange.

"Bellinis, do you think, or simply champagne? Maybe mimosas?" She nudged him. "You're not listening."

Not fully, but thank God for the piece that had been. "Sorry, sweetheart, but my brain jumped to beer."

She laughed then. "That too, but not too much."

And, hell, how long would a divorce take and how soon would Lizbeth want the wedding? That was the one thing they hadn't talked about, and he was reluctant to bring it up until he had more information from Ellie.

"What about my wedding dress? Long or short? Scarlet or jade?"

For a moment, the word hung between them, but that was only in his mind, he knew. For Lizbeth, jade was nothing more than another color, a fancy name for green, like scarlet for red. But, for him, Jade was a forever memory he wished he could erase.

He stood and placed his drink on the table before taking hers and doing the same. Lifting her into his arms, he kissed her and growled, "Long and green for the wedding. Short and red for the wedding night. Or any other damn color and length you want."

Glenn carried her inside and dropped her on the bed, needing the reminder of how good they were together. But, for that first moment, he wasn't holding Lizbeth's slender, almost-but-not-quite too thin frame, but a more rounded, curved body, feeling a heat and a fire he'd never forgotten.

* * *

The next morning, Glenn kept it light on the drive back to the airport where they embraced at the entrance and parted ways for different airlines and different departure gates. He wished now that he'd commandeered the company plane, but there had been trips already on the books, and he wasn't one to pull rank over something as inconsequential as a quick, unplanned weekend trip out of town. Still, the hustle around him rasped on his raw nerves.

At least he'd made Lizbeth happy. He'd remained as relaxed as she needed him to be … as she deserved him to be. Success hadn't made her proud. If anything, it seemed to have humbled her. She was grateful for the opportunities that came her way and worried far too much about letting her agent down. He suspected she worried about letting him down as well.

But once they went their separate ways, frustration swamped him. Having Ellie check his marital status had been more of an afterthought, not something he'd expected to turn into a problem.

And why the hell hadn't the marriage been dissolved? He would have thought an annulment on some Bellamy-bought grounds if not an outright divorce would have been finalized a long time ago. Hadn't that been the purpose of beating the hell out of him and dumping him over the state line?

Or had they simply left him for dead, believed him dead, thinking he'd no longer be a problem for the boss's darling girl?

What ate at him more than anything—or had until he'd moved on—was whether Jade had known what had been done to him. Did she know he'd been barely able to crawl to the highway to flag a car down, not caring if it stopped or ran over him and finished the job that had been started? And that brought him full circle to the question of why they were still married. And to another question. Had she remarried, thinking him dead?

In the first couple of years, she wouldn't have been able to find him. He'd lived payday to payday, always cash, like most of the oil rig roustabouts he worked alongside. He'd slid into Mexico with a foreman who'd taken a liking to the daredevil he'd been. That foreman had passed him on to a higher-up with a word that he'd be one to watch, one to give a chance at a promotion.

When the company moved operations into Central America, Glenn—not quite twenty-one—had moved with it as a foreman with his own crew. More money and he used it wisely. More time off and he used that wisely, too. He came back a decade later, a wealthy man, a self-educated man with multiple degrees from universities with online programs. He was more than wealthy now. If Jade had looked in the few years since he relocated to Florida, she wouldn't have had any problem finding him.

He hated that a part of him wondered, that a part of him wanted to know if she'd cared enough to look. The vulnerable part of him had moved on. He was no longer that kid. But the angry part, that purely male part, yeah, he wanted to know.

Chapter Five

No, Jade thought, the director wasn't happy. Not scowling, as that would have been bad for his public image, but he definitely wasn't pleased to be here.

They exchanged banalities about work and family while a server filled their cups with coffee and placed flatware wrapped in cloth napkins in front of them. Handing them menus, he murmured he'd be back when they were ready to place their orders. Jade gave him a smile and a nod.

When he was out of hearing, Cargill fumbled in his jacket pocket and handed her a business card. "Leo said you needed this."

His fingerprints. Jade slipped it into her briefcase. "Yes, thank you."

Frowning, he leaned back in his seat. "I'm really not

hungry, Jade, and I don't see why this was necessary. We shouldn't be seen together."

"Tell me about the council's plans for the city park renovations and re-opening."

He opened his mouth, closed it again, and gave her as much of a smile as she suspected he could manage. "Is that supposed to distract me?"

"Maybe a little … enough for me to ask a question or two without you having an apoplectic fit. No one is going to think a thing about us having a quick business meeting here. It certainly isn't the first," she reminded.

His shoulders slumped. "I'm sorry. This has been … it's upsetting."

"Of course it is, but if I'm going to be of any help to you, I need what little information you may have without knowing you have it."

"What I know won't take long." He straightened his shoulders before picking up his coffee cup. "Go ahead then."

"Who have you made angry?"

His eyes widened in surprise, then he shook his head. "Angry? No one that I know. Unhappy is a different story."

"So, who have you made unhappy?"

"Every damn person on the city council."

"All at the same time?" She smiled and watched as he let himself relax and smile back.

"No, of course not. They're all good people but deeply divided on most issues. Half oppose progress of any kind, and half advocate change simply for the sake of change."

"And that," Jade said adamantly, "is why I'll never run for public office. I don't have the patience for it. Let's get some food coming while you think beyond the city council for someone who may hold a grudge against you."

The fact that he ordered a full breakfast suggested he was ready for a more hard-hitting line of questions, but she waited until he was nearly finished eating before she broached the subject again.

"Does your sister still hold a grudge?"

For a moment, Cargill avoided her gaze as he put his fork aside and picked up the mug their server had refilled. When he looked up, he sighed. "I'll admit my mind went there at first, Jade, but … no … she's happy now. She realizes she was running with a rough crowd and things were bound to go to hell in a handbasket, as they say. She's in a good place, mentally as well as physically."

"What about the other kids who were in the car that night? Their families?"

"Maybe. But, why now? Why after all this time?"

And that, Jade thought, was a good question and one she'd already asked herself. "Maybe something changed. Maybe one of them isn't in such a great place, mentally or physically."

"Maybe … but wouldn't they be more likely to come after you? You were her voice in front of the judge."

"An advocate, yes, because she was little more than a child while the others were of legal age. But she's your family, your blood; her bond is with you, not me."

He rubbed his jaw. "I suppose I could do some digging."

Jade shook her head firmly. "Too risky for you. Besides, that's my job, remember?"

Pushing his plate aside, he breathed a deep sigh. "And I'm glad it *is* … glad you didn't turn me away. Is there anything else you need to ask? I really need to get to the office."

"Not for now, but I'll be in touch."

* * *

Deep in thought, Jade barely heard the first soft tap at her office door. The second pulled her attention from the information on her screen to the doorway.

Simon shifted anxiously from one foot to the other as she studied him a moment before saying, "Come in."

He took three steps into her office and stopped again. She relaxed against the back of her chair. "Come all the way in and sit down. I'm not going to throw anything at you."

Instead of moving toward her desk, he eased his way into the room and pulled out one of the chairs at the small table she usually kept scattered with papers she didn't want to read. For once, it was empty.

She studied him a moment, then stood and moved from her desk to the table opposite him. She waited, not to make it harder for him, but because she'd found the young male ego to be a fragile thing. He needed to do this his way, not hers.

"I overstepped in speaking to Mr. Colter. I apologize."

"You did," Jade agreed, "but it was less a matter of overstepping than a lack of discretion."

"Ma'am?"

"Not Colter or Jonah or myself are so ego-driven that we'd be offended if someone speaks up out of a real concern. The issue at stake is that you spoke out of turn about something you didn't know enough about. Ours is a business where lives are often at risk and trust is critical."

"Yes, ma'am."

And still, she wasn't sure he understood. "The person who gave me those notes trusted me. That person's life could be at risk. I trusted you. By speaking out, in a hallway no less, by risking being overheard by the wrong person, you could easily have compromised that person's safety." Everyone in the building had security clearances but guests and clients came and went, not freely, but still…

Simon paled and blinked hard behind his glasses. "Robert says you could have me fired."

She relaxed her expression. "Robert also says this is your first mistake. Firing isn't on the table."

At her words, he took a deep breath and his shoulders visibly relaxed, dropping the slightest bit so they, at least, weren't nearly touching his ears.

"You've proven to your supervisor, to Robert, that you're good at what you do. That earned you the promotion you have, the position you're in now."

This time his shoulders squared.

"I accept your apology, but I hope you learn from this," she said. "I'd like to see you emerge as a leader when the opportunity arises."

She stood, and Simon jumped to his feet. "Yes, ma'am. Thank you, ma'am. I'll get back to work now."

"Bring me the fingerprint and handwriting comparisons as soon as you get a response from the Justice Department."

"Me? You want me to report back to you?"

"I do."

"Yes, ma'am." He took a deep breath and nodded. "As soon as possible."

It took courage, she thought as she watched him go, courage to take it beyond a quick apology or, worse, an avoidance of her until the matter was overshadowed by other cases.

And, damn, wasn't she glad she refused direct reports except for an assistant?

* * *

Somehow, she wasn't surprised when Jonah called as she was wrapping up for the day. She'd known Colter hadn't been as satisfied with their conversation as he'd played it.

"Do you have time for coffee? I have something I want to run by you."

She rolled her eyes and thought, sure, something like a lecture. "Downstairs?"

"Let's walk across to that new coffee shop. Best cappuccino ever."

"Fine with me. I'll meet you in the lobby."

When she stepped out of the elevator, Jonah had one shoulder propped against a wall, his gaze fixed on the busy street. Either he'd been warned by the soft sound of the elevator opening or he sensed her presence as she strode toward him.

He turned and his gaze searched her face. "You look tired."

She lifted her brows. "As in haggard?"

He chuckled. "No, as in tired. Like you wouldn't mind a nap."

She smiled and shook her head. "I'm good. Long day but not boring."

"Nothing wrong with boring." He held the door for her as they walked out.

She laughed. "How would we know?"

"We wouldn't," he admitted, chuckling.

They waited at the crosswalk until the light changed, then dashed across all four lanes before it could change again.

Jade drew a deep breath of pleasure as they walked into the coffee shop. It was actually a bit more of a bistro, with a chalk-written menu with the sandwich and pastry of the day, but coffee was the main draw. They ordered and waited at the end of the bar, carrying their coffees and plates to a booth at the back of the seating area.

Always preferring the lead, Jade waited only until Jonah had settled across from her before she spoke. "Colter shouldn't have worried you with this. I've got it handled. I promise."

Jonah leaned back in his chair and took a sip of his coffee. His gaze was steady on her as he asked, "Exactly what is it you have handled?"

She stared at him. "Well, hell."

He grunted and stared right back. "My thoughts exactly. Spill it."

Stifling a sigh, she gave him no more than what she'd given Colter and what she'd thought sure Colter had shared with him … the bare minimum. He wasn't any more impressed than their cousin had been … maybe a little less. He definitely pressed her about the favor she'd done Cargill that had him seeking her out.

"It was a long time ago, and I made a promise to keep silent about it. All I'll say is that it was nothing dangerous, and it was more related to a family member than Cargill himself."

Jonah drummed his fingers on the table as he studied her expression. After a moment, he gave a nod. "I can live with that. I'm not so sure about this blackmail attempt he wants you to handle."

"If that's what it is." She'd said the same to Colter. Both of them were going to be furious down the road, but she'd deal with that when she got down that road.

"That's where it's headed," Jonah said flatly. "You know that as well as I do."

He gazed at the wall behind her as he finished his coffee, then shifted that gaze to her. "You be damned careful and bring us in if things get chancy. I want a promise on that."

She met his gaze steadily. "I promise." And she meant it. She wouldn't like it and would put it off as long as possible, but she wasn't stupid and she didn't have a death wish.

As they were walking toward the door, she stopped. "So, exactly what *was* it you wanted to run by me?"

Jonah rubbed the back of his head. "Oh, yeah, I was thinking about throwing a surprise birthday party for Cheney."

Jade stared at him. "You want my opinion on that?"

"Wouldn't have asked if I didn't," he grumbled.

"Worst idea ever unless you have a sudden death wish." She tilted her head. "Why don't you already know that?"

"Hell, I don't know. I thought something small, family only."

"All thousand of us?" She kept her voice from squeaking.

"No, damn it, just … well, us … you and Colter, Miranda and the boys, Mom and Dad. Not big …." He sighed. "Well, hell, Jade, something special."

She softened. Cheney had no one left that was her own, except them … Jonah who adored her and the family who loved her far beyond the few he mentioned, but those few would be all Cheney could deal with. And maybe Declan Flannery, if anyone could find him. He'd accepted a position with the Slade Agency, but he was like the wind, wild and free and sometimes just as invisible. She took a breath and told herself she was crazy and Cheney would kill her right along with Jonah, but … "I think we could make it work."

She told herself the look on Jonah's face made the risk worth the price. Her family, especially Jonah and Colter, made her crazy, but God in heaven knew she did love them.

Jonah held the door for her and gave her a hug on the sidewalk. "I love you, kid. Be safe, please."

She didn't bother to remind him there weren't that many years between them, just hugged him back and promised she'd do her best. She knew he needed to hear her say it.

They were halfway across the street when she felt the prickling between her shoulder blades. She glanced back and around, but no one and nothing stood out. Beside her, Jonah checked his watch, and she knew he didn't feel anything.

Whoever was watching, wasn't watching him. Jonah would have known, tensed, looked up. As she had.

Chapter Six

Jade lived exactly where and how she chose to live. Her penthouse apartment reflected her life, organized and neat, a far cry from the adventurous, impetuous girl she'd been. She dated infrequently and always on her own terms. No strings, no attachments. Her family was everything and enough.

She returned to the ranch once a month, sometimes for the day, sometimes for the weekend, to ensure her parents were healthy and strong and to saddle her horse and feel the wind on her face. The land called to her with a siren's lure but always let her return to the city, which beat with the pulse of her life.

On this Friday, she walked into her office, planning to leave early and head straight for the ranch. A weekend bag was packed and in the trunk of her car. As much as she loved her job, she needed the time away. With the approach of summer, the days were getting longer. She could leave mid-afternoon and arrive well before dark. She even considered leaving right at noon, but she was still deep into paperwork when Robert tapped on her door not long after.

"Got a minute?"

"Sure, come on in." She smiled, then noticed the folder he carried. "Fingerprint and handwriting comparisons? I thought Simon would bring them."

He returned her smile. "It is, and he would have, but I wanted to talk with you." He moved to sit at the table rather than beside her desk, and she joined him there.

"First, Simon came to see you?"

"And apologized."

"It won't happen again. He scared himself when he realized he could be out of a job."

"There's no shame in making a mistake … only in repeating it."

"At which point, I'd have to take remedial action. He's aware he'll be monitored more closely for a while going forward."

She nodded, satisfied.

With that, Robert opened the folder between them and withdrew both copies of the blackmail notes. "Have there been any others since you were handed these?"

"No, only the two, but I suspect there will be at least one, maybe more. These are like an unfinished thought."

His expression was somber, and his dark eyes thoughtful. "I agree, and I'm sure you won't be surprised that they were written by the same person, but there's no match in the database."

"Not surprised, no."

"What about the fingerprints I forwarded to you?" she asked. "Anything there?"

"Cargill's match the prints on the first note. Yours are a match to those on the second note. There aren't any other matches on either." He rubbed his jaw, looking perplexed.

No surprise there either, she thought as she leaned back in her chair. "I suppose Cargill got wise after the first note and thought about fingerprints with the arrival of the second. As for mine," she grimaced, "I expected both notes to be enfolded within a cover paper. That's not an excuse. It was carelessness on my part." She hated the ongoing lie, but until she knew what was going on, that was the way it would have to be. She wasn't about to have her hands tied by Jonah or Colter. The threat was aimed at her, and she was going to nail whoever had made it.

Robert chuckled softly. "There's not a careless bone in your body. We forget not everyone knows standard operating procedures for our kind of work."

"You wouldn't forget." She said it, and she meant it. Robert never had been nor had he ever tolerated carelessness within his small team. And he never would. He was too steeped in the requirements of the work they did. Although she couldn't share it, she hadn't been either. Still, the possibility existed.

His eyes met hers, and he lifted his chin. "Thank you for that, Jade."

She studied his expression and suspected he'd be blushing if his dark skin allowed for that. And, she thought—since Jonah and Colter insisted she manage the forensics team at least in a general sense—this was as good a time as any to broach a different subject.

"Colter and Jonah and I have been considering an ... I guess you'd call it an expansion. The city has a good forensics lab, but, as you know, we get calls frequently from private businesses, not only in Albuquerque but from across the state, wanting our help. Some of those we pass along to you, but many we don't. We can't. We're not set up for it." She paused. "But we want to be, and we could be."

Robert looked thoughtful. "We could, sure, but it would take changes. Expensive changes."

"Quite a bit," Jade agreed. "In staffing, advanced training, as well as additional equipment and additional management. As for the expense," she shrugged, "we'd recoup that with the requests we now have to turn away." She watched his expression, saw a faint excitement at the possibility of new challenges for his team.

"So, you're thinking of things like ballistics, toxicology, DNA analysis?"

"Maybe even on-site forensics, like fire debris analysis for insurance companies. We've had that call."

He leaned back, and his brow creased faintly. He still seemed excited while clearly trying not to be anxious about the possibility of departmental changes. "We'd need a different team for each of those aspects. Not huge teams initially, but at least a pair."

"That was our thought as well." Expansion of personnel, but carefully, not speedily.

"What can I do to help?"

"I think your first step would be to hire an assistant, then look at what you'd need in additional staffing."

"What I would need?" His voice rose slightly on the word I.

Jade was enjoying herself now. "Well, there are consultants out there, if you want to go that route, but I'll leave that to you. As manager."

"Manager." He said the word softly.

She finally let herself smile. "Congratulations, Robert. You've earned this. Colter and Jonah and I are unanimous on that."

His eyes glittered, and he shifted his gaze away for a moment before turning back to her. "None of you will ever regret this, Jade. I won't let you down. I promise you that."

"And I hope you never regret saying *yes* to the opportunity, Robert. It's a lot to take on, and I'm grateful you're willing. We realize it would be easier on you if you were stepping into a ready-made slot."

He grinned, then. "But to build my own dream team right down to the equipment. Man!"

They talked a few minutes more, then shook hands at the door. Robert was still grinning as he walked out of her office.

Jade took a deep breath. That had felt good in a business where a lot of things went wrong before they were made right. It was a big expansion, maybe even a risky one, but, hell, the entire Bellamy legacy had been built on risk.

* * *

She called Jonah on her way out of town. "About that shindig?"

"Shindig?" he asked cautiously.

"You're private, right?"

"Always."

"Cheney's birthday party … what if we have it at the ranch? An old-fashioned all-day barbecue? She always seems more comfortable there, even with a crowd."

"No crowd," he said empathically.

"I know that already. All I'm saying…"

"I don't know," he sounded hesitant. "I was thinking here in town."

Jade stayed silent, letting him think it through. Town would be good for a fun evening, but Cheney wasn't a fun evening kind of girl. Jonah knew that far better than she did.

Not that Cheney wasn't fun. She was fun and funny as hell, especially if she had a mixed drink. That happened only when she one hundred percent trusted everyone around her, which was rare. But it happened, and Jade, as much as Jonah, wanted it to happen on her birthday.

The mountains, a place that felt like home—a real home—to Cheney, were the only likely place it would.

"Maybe it would be better as far as the twins, too, if we made it a weekend thing," Jonah admitted. "I could take them exploring, maybe rock-hunting." Jade knew he adored Colter and Miranda's sons, his nephews by marriage and by love. "So, you're thinking of your folks' place? Not mine?"

Jade found herself grinning as she answered. "Easier for me to plan. Beyond that, Aunt Eden and I would butt heads over too much." Damn near everything. "She'd win, and you know I hate to lose."

"She can be ... determined."

Jade snorted. Jonah's mother was what most would call a force of nature. She fought as fiercely as she loved.

"And who knows how things will stand between her and Marcus by then."

Marcus and Eden had divorced years ago with the family barely surviving the fiery explosion. They were civil now, but the love between them had never died, and still bubbled with fierce, and fiercely controlled, emotions when they were together.

"There's that, too," Jonah admitted ruefully. "I'll give

you the win on this one, if Aunt Missy and Uncle Calvin are good with it."

"You know they'll be all in." She pushed her luck a little. "So, we're talking my parents, yours, and Colter's along with Miranda and the twins."

"This thing is growing. Don't let it grow to fit the space." Jonah's warning held rueful amusement, but she knew it was still a warning.

"I won't, I promise."

"Your word is good, but I should have made you promise not to make Robert cry."

"He called you? Was he still excited?" If she hadn't been driving, she would have bounced in place.

"I think he was still in shock. Well, double that. I dragged him into the renovations."

"As long as you don't drag me in, you're good." Jade hoped he knew that wasn't a joke. "This is going to take at least an additional floor and we need to keep Robert's team together so that means moving things and personnel around. We're going to have to do some serious juggling."

"You're safe on the renovations. I gave him the name and number of the last architect we used."

"The one who had included the number of nails and screws and nuts and bolts?"

Jonah laughed outright. "That's the one, but that's not why. He also drew up the specs for the bid list but declined to decide who would be placed on the bid list and also declined to evaluate the bids."

"I remember," Jade murmured as she crested the next rise and the ranch came into view. Home, always home. She pulled to the side of the road and gathered her thoughts to finish their conversation. "He had complete neutrality. Yeah, I like it. He's a wise choice."

"Did you know the building next door is tentatively on a bid list?"

"What?" She sat up straight. "Bid? As in to purchase?"

"The architect heard a rumor, and I chased it. It's not a done deal, but it's a possibility."

"We could move forensics there." Her excitement grew. "And the indoor firing range Colter keeps nagging us about."

"So, sounds like you're open to the idea. Do you think we could get it, the firing range, permitted that central to the city?"

She could hear the doubt in his voice, and she smiled. "If we opened it to local law enforcement … free of charge."

"Damn, Jade, that would work."

"First, we have to get the building. So, you'd better get moving before someone else moves faster."

"I've got a better idea. I'll get Dad on it. He's the negotiator."

They talked for a few minutes more, then broke the connection. Jade sat in silence, absorbing the sight of the ranch spread across the valley before her. Her parents still lived in the first home they'd built together. A sprawling single story, it was large but not grand, with a verandah that spanned the front and a screened porch that spanned the back. Every bedroom had a door that opened onto that screened porch and, during the years she'd grown from child to woman, they'd gathered there at the end of each day more often than not.

The original Bellamy Ranch was miles away. As the original three families had grown, they and then their descendants, had purchased every acre that became available around them.

Civilization hadn't left the Bellamys behind, but they hadn't allowed it to encroach upon what was theirs. Not their land, nor their unity, nor their peace. Jade loved the land, loved the mountain, as she loved her family. But she'd come to prefer life in the city. The ranch was a place to come to rest and rejuvenate, but Albuquerque was home now.

The idea of expansion, of doubling their space there, excited her, and her mind raced with ideas. Because the buildings were close, it was possible, even probable, that the architect could design walkways between them at every floor. Maybe a floor in the additional building could be designated as lodging, whether single rooms or mini-apartments for their out-of-town business guests, rather than putting them up in hotels. She pulled out her phone again to make some notes and saw she'd missed two calls from her assistant.

She listened to the first message, frowned because the young woman sounded a little flustered, then put it on speaker as she played it again. "I've forwarded a call that came in on your office line a couple of days ago. I put a transcript on your desk, but it looks as if you moved some papers on top of it. I'm so sorry for not making sure you saw it." She took a deep breath before finishing. "Anyway, I think you may want to return it sooner rather than later. It sounded a little … well, a little odd to me."

Odd? Odd likely meant another intriguing job, another challenge. Feeling a prickle of excitement along her spine, Jade held off until she'd called Lori back and assured her no harm done. Besides, Jade felt she should take the blame … although the threat of blackmail would be a distraction for anyone … not that she said as much.

Finally finished with the reassurances, she touched her

finger to the second message and listened as it played.

The voice was that of a woman, smooth and decidedly southern. "Good afternoon. I'm calling to speak with Jade Bellamy-Davidson. My name is Ellie Keen of Keen & Keen Attorneys-at-Law in St. Petersburg, Florida. I'm calling regarding your legal contract with Glenn Collier. I would appreciate a return call at your convenience."

Chapter Seven

G lenn. Jade stilled as memories chilled her. She hadn't heard his name in well over a decade, closer to two. And that wasn't nearly long enough.

* * *

At eighteen, Jade knew she was lucky, but she wasn't spoiled. She was up before daylight like any other person, young or old, on the ranch. Mornings started with cleaning stalls and saddling horses--hers and her dad's and her mom's. Her brothers took care of their own.

Those brothers, both older, had opted for public school and then college, before returning to the lives they loved at the ranch. She knew there had been miscarriages between them and her, knew her mother had wanted a houseful. Jade might have liked a younger sibling to boss around as those two older brothers bossed her, but—after Jade—the doctors had said 'no more'.

School work was completed around ranching responsibilities ... as long as Jade kept her grades at a B or above. She made damned sure she did because the idea of public school did not appeal.

Those grades were good enough for college, and she thought she might be willing, but classes would be on her terms. Jade liked things on her terms.

The first time she laid eyes on Glenn Collier, he got a good taste of that. Spring and calves had come early. Glenn had ridden in with some of the neighboring ranch hands, just as the Bellamy cowboys would be loaned for a few days here and there during the busy weeks that followed the spring birthing.

The morning air held a chill as they began sorting those calves, separating them from their mothers and gathering them into the branding pen for the few hours it took to vaccinate and brand.

Jade hated the branding, even though her dad made sure the hands knew he wouldn't tolerate the touch of the branding iron taking more than a split second. They were good at their jobs and they were fast, not that they had any particular sympathy for the babies ... but Jade did. She suspected her dad did as well because of how careful his orders were and how closely he watched the process.

From the branding iron, the babies were passed to the vet for salve over the brand and for vaccinations. The harder part was the castration of the little bulls but, unusual for a working ranch, that was done by a local veterinarian who was well-paid for his morning's work on the side of a mountain.

Jade rode her mare expertly, her feet braced in the stirrups against the quick moves it took to keep the calves headed in the right direction. The sun warmed her back as she flopped her hat against her knee, trying to move one of the calves back to the line. The calf chose to be intractable, turning and darting under her mare's belly and the she-cat, as Jade sometimes thought of her horse, decided to pitch a fit.

Jade came off and landed on her backside right in front of Glenn. He stared for a moment, then reached a hand down to help her up.

Instead of taking the hand he held out to her, she scrambled to her feet, embarrassed, muttering, "I'm fine."

He studied her a moment, then turned back to helping push the calves through the gate when they balked at being separated from their mothers.

Jade caught him watching her from time to time through the acrid stink of the branding iron and the frantic bawling of the calves and the softer call of their anxious mothers. He didn't look impressed with her, and she suspected she'd humiliated him by refusing his help as much as she'd been humiliated by being dumped by her horse. One thing her dad demanded of her and her brothers was to show respect to everyone all the time, especially the people who worked for them. If he'd seen, she knew he'd be disappointed in her.

When the cook clanged his ladle against a kettle of hot grease and frying fish, she walked over to where Glenn sat with the other hands and stood in front of him. Talk faded, and several of the hands frowned. Glenn studied her cooly, but she matched that look with a wry smile and a shrug. "I was rude and I apologize. I don't get slung off very often, and it hurt my pride."

"It's okay, ma'am. I don't much like hitting the ground either, but it happens."

The frowns all around faded and talk among the men resumed as she nodded and walked back to sit beside her dad who gave her a silent nod of approval. Slanting another look toward the young hand, she caught him watching her. She couldn't help but notice he was as tall as most of the grown men around him, his shoulders as broad.

That night she dreamed of eyes as dark as coffee and a jaw as strong as her dad's.

* * *

It had taken years for Jade to stop dreaming. She shoved the memories away, thinking hard, not liking what she was thinking. First, the notes that hinted of blackmail to come, then, a name from the most painful part of her past. That was a call she had no intention of returning. She didn't believe in quirks of fate. She never had. If someone wanted to play games, they'd have to increase their effort.

Chapter Eight

Ellie had insisted on coming to him, but Glenn didn't think it was for the reason she gave so he sent his helicopter to pick her up. Sure, most folk enjoyed time in the Florida Keys and she'd made reservations at a nearby resort, but Ellie wasn't a sun and surf fan. She might put her feet up and enjoy the gulf breeze along with a Mai Tai or Manhattan as the mood hit, but she wouldn't be near the sand or salt water and her laptop would be within reach.

He was alerted to her arrival by the sound of helicopter blades and stepped from his office to the wraparound deck.

Sure enough, she carried her laptop as she strode toward the base of the stairs but at least she wasn't in business clothes. A loose, flowery top covered her skinny jeans halfway to the knees. Sparkly earrings dangled far lower than her dark, cropped hair. She glanced up and gave him a quick smile, then focused on keeping her balance as she moved much too quickly up those stairs in heels high enough for a boardroom meeting.

Glenn gave her a smile and took her laptop, placing it on the wide table in front of the sofa. "Drink?"

Her hesitation didn't last more than a second before she nodded. "Yes. Whatever, as long as it's strong."

He took a deep breath. "That doesn't sound promising."

"No, not promising, but not catastrophic."

Nodding, Glenn waved toward the living area. "Get comfortable. I'll mix the drinks." Or rather, he'd mix hers. He had a feeling his liquor might be better straight up.

Moments later, he placed a fresh Mango Margarita in front of her and took the side chair opposite the couch watching as she worked quickly on her computer.

"And you're doing what…?"

"Sending a document to your printer." She leaned back and picked up her drink with a long inward breath of appreciation. "This looks amazing."

"And what does your document look like?" Glenn asked dryly.

"Like an offer."

He slowly lowered the glass in his hand without taking a drink. "Of what?"

She sighed. "Not to sue for her millions, if she doesn't sue for yours."

"I don't want anything she has."

"Maybe not but do you want her to have anything you've created from nothing?"

"So, she's threatened?" He didn't bother to hide his disgust.

Ellie drank from her frost-rimmed glass and sighed.

"I'll probably need another of these before we're done." Then she shook her head. "She hasn't threatened anything. She hasn't returned phone calls or email. Her staff simply says she's unavailable at the current time."

Her staff. Glenn tried to picture the fiery, head-strong girl he'd known seated behind a desk. But maybe that was the wrong image. Maybe her staff encompassed no more than a social secretary, makeup artist, and hairdresser. God knows her family had the wealth to keep her in the style to which she'd been born.

"So, it's only been a few days, right?"

"Long enough for her to have returned my calls if she had any intention of doing that."

Glenn had no reason to argue the point. He gritted his teeth then forced himself to relax. Ellie was right in that there was no point in dragging this out, even though Lizbeth wasn't pressing for a wedding date. Her own schedule had her tied up for weeks more, and there was the planning and arranging to do. She didn't want grand, but she did want perfect. And Glenn wanted that for her. She would make a good wife, and together they would make a good marriage.

"Fine. I'll sign the document."

"Nothing to sign until she reads and agrees."

His fingers tightened around his drink until he forced himself to relax them. No need to break perfectly good glassware.

"So, what do you suggest? If she's ignoring phone calls, she'll as likely ignore mail."

Ellie gave him her courtroom look. "She won't ignore me."

"You intend to go to her? Damn, Ellie. That's half a continent away."

"I think it's wise if you want to get married anytime this year."

"So, if she signs," and maybe she wouldn't if she did her homework first, "what are the requirements for divorce in the state?"

"New Mexico? There's a residency requirement; at least one spouse must have lived in the state for at least six months and must have a domicile there. She meets that. Then there's a thirty-day waiting period after the papers are filed."

"Can the waiting period be waived?" Not that it would need to be if Jade agreed to sign the papers without a fight.

"It can be, and likely would be, considering how long the two of you have been physically separated." Her brow furrowed. "The only hitch would be if she has an inkling of what you're worth."

"It can't be a fraction of what the Bellamys have behind them."

"No, it isn't, but the Bellamy money, by and large, is tied up in land and livestock, in buildings and in businesses and employees. No one is lacking for *anything* they need and *little* they might want, but none of them can take a chunk of it and walk away to do their own thing."

And Glenn knew, for some there would always be an allure to that. For Jade? Once he could have said with no hesitation that wouldn't appeal to her. But the Jade he knew was eighteen. He knew nothing about the woman she was now.

And with that thought, swiftly and unexpectedly, came the realization that he wanted to see her. He wanted to look her in the eye. He wanted to see her put her signature on the paper that would dissolve the last tie between them.

"Cancel your reservations and stay here through the

weekend. I'm going to Albuquerque. I'll take the damn papers with me."

Ellie took a deep breath. "I don't know if that's a wise thought."

For a moment, Glenn stared past her at the gulf waters that danced and splashed in the late afternoon sun, then shifted his gaze back to her. "It's the only one I have at the moment."

She nodded, not looking happy. "Tonight?"

"No, tonight I'm getting drunk. I'll fly out tomorrow."

"Can't say as I blame you there." She hesitated, then said sincerely, "You're a good person, Glenn, and I hate that I can't make this go away, that I can't make it any easier."

He got to his feet. "I'll want the jet for Albuquerque. I'll get your things and send the pilot and helicopter home."

"I hate to impose on your staff."

"The guest suite is always ready, and my cook will be glad to have someone who appreciates fine wine and good food. He complains that I am not that person."

She chuckled. "Well, Wesley and I happen to know you are … as long as the wine is red and the steak is rare."

He forced a smile. "That husband of yours knows exactly how long to leave a T-bone on the grill."

"Speaking of which. I'd better let him know my change of plans."

"Hell, why don't you have him join you and extend your stay?"

"I might do that." She smiled, but Glenn still saw the sympathy in her eyes as he turned to go.

Maybe, he thought, he'd take a stroll along the beach until she had time to get busy with work as he knew she would. He didn't need or want sympathy. He wanted to hold on to his anger. He wanted Jade to pay.

* * *

The following morning, Glenn settled into the flight, glancing at the seat beside him occupied only by his briefcase. At the moment, it was as tangible as a living, breathing entity because it held the information Ellie had collected on Jade and her family, and it held their divorce papers. He'd open it soon. For now, he let it mock him. At least he didn't have a hangover.

When he'd returned from his beach walk the afternoon before, Ellie had laid claim to his dining table with papers and folders strewn everywhere. She'd asked if he wanted to review the information on Jade, and he had declined. He trusted her to have been as thorough in that as she was in everything else.

Instead, they had talked Collier Oil business ... drilling and investments. Anything but Jade and Lizbeth and his impending divorce and second marriage. Reminded of all the good things he had going in his life, he hadn't felt the need to reach for a bottle, much less drain it.

Unfortunately, at the moment, while sobriety meant a clear head for the information he had to absorb, it also meant no barrier to the sting of his past mistakes. The first of which had been falling for a dark-eyed girl who could ride a horse and throw a rope as well as any of her father's ranch hands and, perhaps, marginally better than either of her brothers.

The first paper he pulled from his briefcase was her current financial status. He was impressed, but he wasn't surprised. He would've liked to tell himself it was all her family's doing, but he never lied to himself. Jade's mind had been as sharp and skilled with thinking things through as her body had been with reflexes.

The more he read, the more that proved an accurate assessment. She'd completed high school while wrangling horses and cattle on her parents' ranch. She'd completed college while working full-time as an intern in several facets of the Bellamy empire, from accounting to research to fieldwork. Currently, she and two of her cousins headed up the Slade Agency. He was familiar with the name, had heard it mentioned in newscasts, but not associated it with the Bellamy conglomerate. No reason he would have.

Once he'd healed from the beating he'd been given—and that had taken months—he'd worked hard to put it all behind him. He hadn't needed the warnings he'd been given as he lay face down on the ground staring at their boots. He'd barely registered the threats of what would happen to him if he ever set foot back in New Mexico.

None of that had mattered. Nothing had mattered after being told Jade knew she'd made a mistake taking up with an outsider, someone who couldn't give her the things a Bellamy daughter deserved. Those were the very things that had made him treasure her. That she trusted him to take care of her even though they were young, even though they hadn't known each other long. That she loved him more than her family's wealth. Until she hadn't.

He pushed the thoughts away. The sting of loss had long since faded. Now there was only the burn of regret that he'd been so naïve. The disgust that he'd been so trusting.

Taking a steadying breath, he kept reading.

Her parents were still living, still together as so many were not … as he once thought to be with Jade. More fool, he. Interestingly, her older brother by a year had been killed in a rockslide years ago. Glenn studied the article for several minutes. There wasn't much there, but something about it nudged hard at a memory long buried.

Buried but not forgotten, the image stark. The mountainside with its scattering of piñon and juniper. The body, already stiff, falling from an outcropping of shale and limestone, tumbling end over end. That downward spiral surrounded by an eerie light. Memory or nightmare? He had never been quite sure after all that had happened, being beaten unconscious had muddied the waters.

Silas's death had been different, though. He'd gone out that morning alone, searching for a bull that failed to come in with the herd the previous day. His horse, still saddled, returned to the ranch at feeding time. It had taken them three days to find him in the bottom of a gully, mostly buried by rock and underbrush.

Silas's younger brother, Morgan, was three-times-divorced with three sons, one from each of the marriages.

As far as the world was concerned, Jade had never married. As far as Glenn was concerned, he wished like hell that lie was true.

He lingered longest over the photographs, studying them one at a time. There weren't many, but there were enough. It felt surreal watching her age from the young girl he'd married to a poised woman he didn't know at all. None of the pictures would be standard fare for most young women, even those with rising stars. Not one in cap and gown, neither high school nor college, though she had the degrees. None at debutante balls or society luncheons.

The earliest would, he thought, have been about the time he met her. One of the Bellamy ranches had been featured in a tourist magazine for the state. There were two action shots of Jade, one astride a horse, herding a group of young cattle into a round pen. The other as she put heels to her horse, swinging a coiled rope intended for the young calf who must have slipped away from the others. Jade's dark hair was loose beneath her hat, whirling about her shoulders and gleaming in the sun. The photographs were silent, but her face reflected the excitement of open air, bawling cattle, and shouting cowboys.

There were others, some years apart, as she met with city leaders or was interviewed by local reporters or television hosts. Business attire suited her trim figure, and she looked as comfortable in that as she did in her ranch gear. A Bellamy through and through. She'd even dropped her father's surname. She wasn't Mrs. Collier, but she was no longer Miss Bellamy-Davidson. She'd made her place, and she was *the* Jade Bellamy of Albuquerque, New Mexico.

He shifted uncomfortably, as he wondered if she sounded the same, smelled the same. At eighteen, she'd smelled of sun and wind. Her later photographs made a statement for expensive perfumes. He forced himself to relax his grip on the images and put the last of them back in his briefcase. Turning to stare out the window as the plane began its descent toward Albuquerque, he wished like hell he had a drink.

But if he knew anything about anything, it was that he'd need to be stone-cold sober to deal with what lay ahead.

Chapter Nine

Jade brought her bags down, then went in search of her mother. She and her dad had shared a pot of coffee earlier. Jade knew her mother had deliberately given them that time alone, as she always did when Jade came home. Her father had headed out to saddle up, and now, she and her mother would have their time.

She stepped out onto the back porch, and her mother smiled at her from the old wooden swing. Jade joined her there. For a few minutes, she was back in time as they sat without speaking, enjoying the peace.

"You should stay for breakfast."

Jade chuckled. "Mama…"

"I know," Melissa, or Missy as her friends knew her, grinned, "if you stayed for breakfast, I'd suggest you stay for lunch, then maybe for dinner as well." Her grin faded to a faint smile. "Albuquerque seems so far away."

"You know it isn't. You could come once a week and have lunch with me and be home by dinner."

They both knew she wouldn't. Missy Bellamy-Davidson was as much a homebody as her husband. Not that there was a dowdy bone in her body. There wasn't. Missy had a sense of fashion and a classiness that came naturally to her. And she had a stubbornness her husband had yielded to when she'd insisted that she, as well as their children, would always carry the surname Bellamy along with her married name of Davidson.

"I worry about you, Jade. I know you're capable, but there's so much ugliness in the world today." She hesitated. "The papers reported another missing person. I didn't hear about the first, and I guess I didn't pay enough attention to the second report, but they stressed this one had similarities to both."

"Newspapers are in the stressing business. The more stressed the readers, the more news sells."

"Different connotations," Missy retorted, her tone semi-exasperated.

"But accurate in either regard," Jade said. "Besides, I'm trained and capable and careful. You know that."

"I do." But her mother still didn't look or sound happy.

Jade leaned her head against the shoulder that had listened to her young hopes and dreams until the day she'd stopped sharing, the day she'd fallen in love. "I love you, Mama," she said softly.

"I know, baby girl. I know you do."

As she carried her bag to her car, she realized that each time she left, she worried a bit more about her parents, as much or maybe more than they worried about her. When, she wondered, had the tables turned? Was it simply a factor of growing up or was it also a part of the work she did, of seeing some of the worst of humanity walking the streets and doing harm where they would?

At a different time in her life, she would have talked with them about the blackmail notes, if that's even what they were. Now? Now, she was as capable, likely more so, of taking care of herself than they were.

* * *

A few mornings later, she sat at a conference table with her cousins, studying that missing person report. This was the third in three weeks. The city police leaned toward a serial kidnapper, and—as of the last disappearance the week before—they wanted the Slade Agency in on the case, unofficially, of course.

With no bodies yet found, there was still hope. With each day that passed without a ransom demand, that hope faded.

Colter and Jonah had already dissected the backgrounds and home lives of the victims in all three cases but couldn't find any link other than commonalities. All were female, all worked in the same building but not for the same employer and all went out around lunchtime each workday but never together as far as coworkers and building security were aware. And none had come back to work or returned home. Security cameras caught each of them walking away from the building alone, then disappearing into the lunchtime crowd. None of them had the same build or hair color or sufficiently similar facial features to attract someone with a fetish. Their ages ranged from twenty-four to fifty-seven.

"It's possible they all went to meet the same person.

An online stalker, maybe? Someone who reached out to them on social media. Someone whose fake profile looked like a regular Joe with a regular job?"

Colter shook his head. "We've dug into social media accounts for each of them, business-sponsored as well as personal ones. There's nothing."

"And no hits on banks or credit cards?"

Jonah's expression was grim as he answered, "Nothing."

Jade drummed her fingers as she stared at the papers scattered around them and, *finally*, something caught her attention, a long shot, but ... "Guys?"

Her tone made them both sit straight and look at her. "The first disappeared on a Monday, the second on Tuesday ..."

Before she could finish, Colter said, "and the third on Wednesday."

"And tomorrow is Thursday." Jonah took a deep breath, adding, "We need a plan, and fast."

None of them questioned why that pattern. That was a shrink's job, not theirs. Their job was to break the pattern.

* * *

There was, Glenn thought, little privacy in a free society. In this instance, he didn't mind as the fact worked in his favor. At his request, Ellie had obtained and sent the make and model of Jade's car, the name and location of her apartment building, Bellamy owned, and that her office was located in the Bellamy Building.

He'd spent the first couple days observing her comings and goings. That wasn't his usual straightforward method of operation, but this wasn't a business deal. He had no intention of walking into her office, surrounded by her kin, and handing her divorce papers, which she likely wouldn't sign without an attorney going through them first.

If it came to a battle, they'd fight, but they'd do it in court, not on her home turf.

Still, he wanted to see her, he wanted to catch her off-guard and read her expression. He hoped he shocked the hell out of her. He hoped a lot of things, but all he really needed was to leave with her signature on those papers.

A few minutes before seven, he parked across the street and several doors down from her apartment building, to watch and wait. An hour from now, the street would be full, but it was quiet at the moment. If Jade held to her pattern, she'd walk the few blocks to the Bellamy headquarters.

She didn't. She pulled out of the parking garage half an hour after he parked. With a quick motion, he started his rental and pulled in behind her, slowed to make room for one car to pass, then tailed. Not too close, but close enough.

He frowned when she passed the Bellamy headquarters and took the ramp onto the interstate. A short distance later she took the first exit, still part of the business district, he thought, but a less prosperous area showing some age and maybe a little neglect. Not seedy, but almost.

When she turned at the end of the ramp, he eased his foot off the gas, letting a sports car cut in front of him. She parked in front of a building with a professionally crafted sign that read 'Office Space For Rent. Inquire inside'. He pulled into the parking area between that building and the next, and he waited. He didn't theorize about her purpose there. It didn't matter … hair appointment, nails buffed and polished, yoga session, destroying an opponent's future. He had no doubt that she—that any of the Bellamy descendants—would destroy anyone in their way without blinking an eye.

The morning passed with excruciating slowness, but Glenn forced himself to sit patiently behind the wheel of the nondescript rental. He made use of his time by calling the crew lead on each of his oil rigs and then his office lead before ending with Ellie.

"Have you talked with her?"

He smiled. No banalities for Ellie. Always straight to the point business.

"Not yet."

"What the hell, Glenn? What are you waiting for?"

"We're about to have our first encounter."

"That sounds a little ominous." She hesitated, and when he didn't speak, he heard her sigh. "Don't do anything stupid. I don't mind posting bail, but I'm not a defense attorney."

"I won't need one." As movement caught his attention, he added, "I'll be in touch," and broke the connection before she could answer.

Jade stepped out and strode past her car and then the lot where he was parked. It seemed he'd been accurate in guessing her purpose. Her hair was wrapped around her head in a completely different style. One he didn't think suited her. Not that it mattered. He eased open his car door and followed, closing the gap between them with swift but silent steps.

Jade was passing near the entrance of what appeared to be an abandoned parking garage, when a man stepped out between them, focused on Jade initially then froze as if sensing Glenn's presence. He looked over his shoulder at Glenn, then faded back the way he'd come. Glenn frowned before returning his focus to Jade. Weird, he decided, but not his problem as long as the guy didn't get between him and his soon-to-be ex-wife.

Before Glenn had time for another thought, all hell broke loose. Tackled from two directions, he gave as good as he got. He had the satisfaction of planting his fist against a solid jaw, before whirling to catch the other guy behind the knee with a sweep of his right leg. He might have taken both of them down if he hadn't heard the familiar sound of a pistol being cocked.

He stilled as his arms were jerked behind him. His gaze met Jade's, and he smiled grimly as her eyes widened and the color drained from her face. She lowered the hand holding the gun until it dangled at her side.

"I see you still have your goons at the ready." He shot one a look. "Sorry if I don't recognize you, but I was at a disadvantage last time around. The odds were the same. Two of you, one of me. But, back then, you came at me from behind and in the dark. After, well … it's hard to pull off a blindfold with your arms—one of them fractured—tied behind you."

The guy who held Glenn's right arm pinned behind his back turned to Jade. "You know him?"

In almost the same instant, the man restraining his left arm asked, "Who the hell are you?"

Glenn fixed his gaze on Jade's face. "Her husband."

* * *

Jade fought to keep her teeth from chattering. She'd quit dreaming of Glenn years ago, the sweet dreams that left her weeping when she awakened to reality, the nightmares when she woke rigid with fury and self-loathing and the inevitable regret.

Colter said her name softly, and, her gaze still locked

with Glenn's, she nodded.

Jonah grunted. "Let's get off the street, shall we?" He glanced at Glenn and cautiously released his arm. "You got a name?"

"Collier. Glenn Collier."

Colter studied him a moment. "Collier Oil?"

He rotated his shoulder and nodded.

"Well … hell." Jonah said as he, too, released his grip and stepped back. "I guess slinging you off the overpass wouldn't be the best idea."

Colter gave him the once-over and flexed his knee. "Damn, but you fight dirty."

Glenn rubbed his wrist. "I learned—not early enough—but I learned."

Jade turned and walked away, not so much as glancing back when Jonah called after her, "My office."

When she reached her car, she dropped the pistol and her cell phone into the storage compartment between the front seats. She was miles away and still driving when the phone stopped ringing.

Chapter Ten

A part of him was surprised Jade had recognized him. Another part knew he would have recognized her anytime and anyplace, even if he hadn't watched her transition from teen to woman through the photographs Ellie had sent.

Glenn glared at the two men who'd tried to take him down and might well have succeeded. "Now that you know my identity, maybe you'd return the favor."

"Jonah Slade." Slade lifted his chin at the other man. "And Colter Bellamy."

"I'd say it was nice to meet you, but…" Glenn let the situation speak for him.

Bellamy rubbed his jaw. "You pack a punch."

Glenn eyed him for a moment. "Care to tell me why

the two of you made it necessary?"

They exchanged glances, and Slade answered. "If you'll come back to the office and explain why you were in this particular place at this particular time, why you felt the need to lie in wait for Jade, we'll answer your question."

After a moment, Glenn nodded. These two seemed his best—if not his only—access to Jade. At least not without a hell of a lot of effort, considering she might well keep running until she knew he was gone.

"I suppose you know where the Bellamy Building is." It wasn't a question.

"I do." With that, he turned on his heel and walked away.

Still, instead of taking the lead, he waited until Bellamy pulled out of a parking space a block up the street. He checked his rearview mirror and saw that Slade had appeared behind him, successfully sandwiching his car between the two cousins. After thinking about it a couple of blocks, he acknowledged this was the only way he was going to get the answers he needed so he continued in the caravan to the parking garage of their office building.

A uniformed guard stepped out of a glass enclosure, smiled and handed him a bright tag with a clip. "Welcome, Mr. Collier, Mr. Jonah said you were visiting for the day. If you would, place this on your visor or anyplace easily visible from the exterior. That will keep our hourly patrol from wasting my time with a report on your vehicle."

Glenn clipped the tag to his visor. "No problem." He couldn't have cared less about their hourly patrol, but he was being treated with dignity so he'd return the favor.

"Thank you, sir." With that, the guard stepped back.

The parking spaces were all large, and Glenn pulled in next to one of the trucks he'd been following. Once upon a time, he would have been impressed by 'family-owned' buildings. Those days were far in the past. He owned several himself, and, yes, one—the first—still bore his name. But his pride wasn't in that building or in his wealth. His only pride came from the fact that he'd built something from nothing … less than nothing.

The other two men waited at the elevator. He stepped in without comment, then followed them out when the doors slid open, not bothering to see what floor they were on. They walked in silence down a hallway with one side of solid windows that looked across the rooftops of the buildings around them.

Slade murmured something to the receptionist as they passed, then they followed him into a conference room where he closed the door behind them. Bellamy gestured toward a chair as he took one across the table. Slade went to the far end and rubbed his hand over his face before looking up at Glenn.

"I'll be damned if I even know where to start."

"Well, I do," Glenn said with an edge. "I'm engaged to be married, and I need Jade's signature on divorce papers."

"You thought accosting her from behind in a sketchy neighborhood was the way to go about getting that signature?" Slade stared across the table at Glenn. "Besides, you should have thought about that before you got engaged."

The sarcasm in his voice hit a nerve, and damned, Glenn thought, if it wasn't his last one. "If I'd had any idea that Jade and I were still married, I would have done that a long time ago, Mr. Slade. What was the point of me being damned-near killed and dumped across the state line, if it wasn't to ensure the darling of the family was free from what clearly was considered a mistake?"

The other man leaned back, his head tilted slightly. "So you say. How come no one knows anything about this so-called marriage?"

"You heard Jade. Or don't you believe her?" Glenn asked.

Some of the tension eased from his posture as he said, "Well … damn." He clenched then unclenched his jaw. "Hell, you may as well call me Jonah and him Colter," he nodded toward Bellamy. "For now, at least, it appears we're family, and, regardless, mister this and mister that tends to get old … unless I'm using it to intimidate," he added with an unexpected grin.

"I don't intimidate easily," Glenn countered.

"I suspected that much without help, Mr. Collier."

Glenn shrugged, accepting their first name status. "It's Glenn."

"And you live in the Keys, if memory serves."

"I guess it serves fine, as you're correct."

"I read the feature article on your company in the last Kiplinger; Collier Oil is predicted to go global by the end of the decade."

That wasn't Glenn's plan, but plans could change. He didn't comment, and Slade didn't seem to expect one.

"For the moment, let's put aside the fact that you claim you were forced to leave, and you believe it was Jade's family that did the forcing and that you'd long since thought the marriage dissolved by whatever means. Let's start with you discovering you weren't," he tilted his head, "which was how?"

"Not wanting to commit bigamy, I had my attorney check, to be sure."

"What a nasty surprise." The comment came from the other end of the table, and Glenn turned to look at Colter.

He expected a sarcastic expression. The hint of sympathy caught him off guard.

"Not what I expected."

"So, you've got a girlfriend back in Florida, thinking you're about to get married."

"Fiancée," Glenn corrected.

"Does she know about this unexpected hitch?"

"No, and I don't plan to tell her until it's resolved and no longer a problem."

Colter appeared to ponder that but didn't argue the point. Not that it would have mattered if he had. Glenn didn't consider it anyone's business but his and Jade's. He was answering their questions for now, but he'd do that only to a point, and then he'd be done.

"Why not have your attorney send the papers over for her to sign?"

Jonah's question was logical, but Glenn wasn't sure he had a logical answer. At least not one he wanted to admit to these two. So, he gave one that wasn't a lie but was far from the whole truth. "All things considered, I thought it best to be sure it was really done."

Colter nodded, but Jonah studied him a moment before he took a different track. "So, I suppose after you arrived in Albuquerque, you watched her for a few days, long enough to figure out her comings and goings and thought you'd surprise her into signing."

"Doesn't sound as smart as I thought when put into words."

"Probably wasn't, but I might have done the same in your shoes."

Jonah's admission surprised him, and Jonah gave a grunt of laughter at Glenn's expression.

"I'd like to know more about the beating you say you took."

Glenn cut Colter a look. "I'll let Jade fill you in on that."

"You're assuming she knew."

Glenn hadn't any doubt, but he shrugged. "I kept my end of the bargain. It's your turn. If you didn't know I was trailing Jade, if you weren't watching me, why were you watching her after what I'm guessing was a hair appointment?"

"It was a hair appointment, of sorts, but not her usual style, not her usual place, and not for obvious reasons." He hesitated. "Three women have been reported missing after visiting that building, one per week in the last three weeks. The first on a Monday, the second on a Tuesday, the third on a Wednesday."

Today was Thursday. Glenn shifted his gaze from one to the other, initially stunned, then furious. "You set Jade up as effing bait? Your own cousin? And where was the police surveillance?"

"We were surveillance," Jonah growled. "And if we hadn't taken you down, the APD sniper on that roof would have taken you out."

"And Jade set herself up," Colter inserted calmly. "She's smart and as skilled as any of us with any firearm you care to name. Not to mention she's kickass in martial arts. She's not the kid you say you married. And who the hell would agree to marry the two of you at ... what? Seventeen?"

"Eighteen." Glenn corrected, hanging on to his patience. Only by a few weeks, but still.

"As if that makes any damned difference."

"Regardless, it happened, and it was legal, and I'd have her signature on divorce papers by now if the two of you hadn't been playing cops and robbers. And some asshole could've had his hands on her if I hadn't been there." He stilled, caught by a quick memory, barely more than a flash of an image. "Wait. That old parking garage … the guy that stepped out, then moved back in when I noticed him, when he saw me … did you see him?"

"What man? Damn it! He was there?" Colter's voice held a wealth of frustration.

"No way to know if he was your guy," Glenn reminded, "but, yeah, I saw someone, and he didn't look happy to see me."

Jonah held his hand up. "You saw him? His face?"

"Face, build, clothes."

Jonah pulled his cell phone and placed a call. "This is Jonah Slade. I need the chief or next in charge. Whoever is there." He stood and paced the room as he waited, then as he talked. When he broke the connection, his expression was one of grim satisfaction. "A police artist will be here in ten or less." He turned to Glenn. "Want coffee?"

"Might as well," Glenn agreed. "Sounds like it's going to be a long afternoon."

Jonah made another call, asking for coffee and sandwiches.

* * *

A long afternoon and not nearly as easy as they made it appear in the movies, Glenn thought, as the chief of police and his detective paced in the background, although made far easier by the use of technology. When he described a broad forehead, the first rendition could have been a young Tom Cruise when the reality was more Neil Patrick Harris who, the artist shared, had been born right there in

Albuquerque, which fact seemed of interest to her but was none to him. From there, she lengthened and narrowed the jawline at Glenn's direction. She changed the arched eyebrows from an inner arch to more of a centered one. What Glenn called a pointed ear, the artist explained was actually a narrow one. The close-set eyes hadn't been easy, but the thin nose proved hardest to nail down. She quickly added sparse hair, cut short and dark brown like his eyes.

From there the focus shifted to his height, the width of his shoulders—which were narrow—his hands, larger than Glenn's was the best he could describe, with fat fingers.

Clothing proved easy, faded jeans and a plain, long-sleeved faded gray tee shirt, but little use in the long run.

When they finished, the artist leaned back and looked at Glenn. "Done?"

"Done."

But apparently, she wasn't. "Now, close your eyes, see his face, his jaw, his neck. Anything stand out?"

Glenn opened his eyes and almost smiled. "You mean what did I miss focusing on his eyes, ears, and nose?" She was good, damned good. "A mole right at the neckline of his tee shirt, my right, so his left. It's large but light-colored. Almost the same shade as his tee shirt, in fact."

"Gray … possible melanoma," she murmured, before asking, "Anything else?"

Glenn shook his head as he stared at the image she'd created with no more than his words. It seemed like enough to him, but then he'd seen the guy and knew how well she'd done her work. He stood and stretched while the chief studied the image, then beckoned the detective to one corner of the room. The artist repacked her sketch pad, pencils, and computer into her shoulder bag. Moments later, she walked out with the detective, and the chief crossed the room to shake Glenn's hand.

"I appreciate your time, Mr. Collier. We'll have this image out to our officers in the next few minutes and it will hit the internet and local television stations soon after. We're damned lucky you happened to be in the area when these guys set their trap." He shifted his attention from Glenn to Jonah. "I'd hoped Jade would join us, but make sure she knows how much I appreciate her efforts this morning."

And that, Glenn thought, as he found himself alone with Jade's cousins once more.

Jonah pulled a decanter and three glasses from a cabinet and sat one in front of Glenn with a soft thud. "We owe you." He poured all of them a small measure, and for a few minutes, they sat in companionable silence, giving Glenn a glimpse of what might have been his future had things been different. High profile, affluent, with a wife who went around busting men's balls. Bad guys, yeah, but still. Jade had put her life in jeopardy, which irked him even though they'd soon be divorced and she'd be free to carry on doing whatever dangerous shit she wanted.

"You two do the work of the local law often?"

"We work *with* them frequently." Colter leaned back in his chair studying Glenn. "As for Jade, she makes her own decisions."

Glenn picked up his glass and stared at it a moment before taking a drink and setting it down again. It wasn't often that strangers were able to read him that easily. Rarely, in fact. He didn't like that these two had. As close as they might be to Jade, they were strangers to him.

"I don't remember either of you," he said at last.

"I'd have to say the same," Jonah admitted.

Colter grunted agreement. "How many years were you

at the Davidson place?"

"Their ranch?" Glenn shook his head. "I wasn't. I'd been with a neighboring ranch for a few months before I met her."

"But they let you marry their daughter at eighteen? And none of us ever heard of it?" Jonah sounded dubious as hell.

Glenn snorted. "Neither did they. Or so I thought."

"Sounds like the Jade I remember," Colter commented.

"But not the Jade she is now?"

Colter contemplated the question a moment. "She's still headstrong, but she doesn't rush her fences now. She's older, and she's smarter." He shrugged. "Hell, we all are."

Glenn couldn't tell if he was included in that or not, then decided it didn't matter either way. He'd been street smart and savvy enough to build a company from the ground up. He might not be able to buy and sell a single Bellamy, but if he sat down at a table to negotiate a deal with them, he wouldn't come out with the short end of the stick.

Chapter Eleven

For the first hour or so, Jade could not have said what she thought or how she felt. As she closed the distance between herself and the ranch, a sense of emptiness made her heart ache. The same emptiness she'd felt when they told her Silas's body had been found. Silas, who had taught her to swing, to rope, and to ride. To take care of herself. Her father had coddled her and would have smothered her had it not been for Silas.

The same emptiness she'd felt when she found the letter Glenn had written and left on her pillow the day he'd walked away. He was sorry. They were too young. He needed a few more years of freedom before he'd be ready to settle down with a wife. The idea of supporting a wife, maybe even a family if they weren't careful, scared him.

Maybe he'd be back someday.

Maybe not emptiness at first, she thought now. She'd screamed before the screams faded to sobs, and the sobs to quiet, cold rage. It was that cold that had carried her through. It made the pretending easier, or—if not easy, at least possible. Pretending to her family. Pretending to herself.

Years had passed, and she had healed. But now, in this moment, with the highway miles ahead and behind, she didn't feel healed. She felt bruised and raw after looking into his eyes, hearing his voice.

I see you still have your goons at the ready.

It's hard to pull off a blindfold with your arms—one of them fractured—tied behind you.

Her mind pushed back on his words, rejected them. Lies. His lies. Nothing else was tenable.

Without a conscious decision, her foot eased on the gas pedal, slowing for nearly a mile before she pulled to the shoulder and laid her forehead against the steering wheel.

Instinctively, she'd sought the peace of the ranch, still a few miles ahead of her. Or maybe she was running from answers because ... what if?

* * *

Jade let her mare pick her way toward the base of the mountain. Trix was young, only five, but as solid as any horse on the ranch. Her father had selected her for Jade's fifteenth birthday, and Silas had trained her. Some ranchers held that geldings were better for ranch work. That mares were too flighty, too likely to 'go off the rails' if they found themselves in a bind. Her father disagreed vehemently with that line of thought. He never rode anything but mares, and neither did his sons. Nor would his daughter.

Although Jade talked to Trix as she rode, her mind wasn't altogether with the mare. It was already at the lake, which was so not where she was supposed to be headed that morning. She'd left a note for her mother. "The trout are calling to me. I'll bring back dinner." But it wasn't the thought of fried trout that called nor the joy of casting a lure.

Glenn waited, his gelding standing motionless next to him, ground-tied. She saw Glenn before he spotted her. He had one shoulder propped against a boulder and, the instant he caught sight of her, his lips curved and his eyes darkened in a way she could never have explained or described but felt deep within her soul. When she'd begun the transition from child to woman, her mother had cautioned her not to trust her first thoughts on a boy but to give herself time. She'd warned of hormones, normal and persuasive. Wait, she'd urged. Wait until you're sure.

Jade was sure.

She touched the reins lightly, signaling her mare to stop. As Glenn reached for her, she leaned forward into his arms. She couldn't imagine anyone feeling the way she did in that moment.

They'd been so young, so in love. So naïve. Jade hit her head lightly against the steering wheel three times, sighed, then turned the car around.

* * *

Glenn stared out across the city from a top-floor hotel suite. He'd been offered a guest apartment in one of the several company buildings. He'd declined. He had, however, accepted a dinner invitation. More, he told himself, out of curiosity than anything else.

Restless, he checked the time, then called Ellie.

"Hey, boss, how's it going? Papers signed?"

"Not exactly."

There was silence, then, "Actually, that's a yes or no question."

He sighed. "I know." Then he told her what had happened. All of it.

The silence was longer this time. "So, these cousins," she put a slight emphasis on the word, "never heard of you, didn't know you from Adam … the original that is … and your wife stomped the gas heading out to God knows where."

Glenn fought simultaneous urges to curse and to hit his head against a wall, so he did all that was left to do in some situations. He laughed. "That sums it up."

"What now?"

"Tonight, I'm having dinner with the cousins. Tomorrow?" He shrugged, even though she couldn't see it. "I guess tomorrow I'll try to chase down my wife. I can't imagine she'd refuse once the shock wears off."

"Glenn …" her voice softened, and his neck tensed in response. He didn't want or need sympathy. What happened was decades in the past. He was long since over whatever they'd had. They probably wouldn't have lasted anyway. "What if she didn't know?"

At his silence, Ellie persisted. "What if she thought you ran out on her?"

He'd thought about the possibility as they'd stared each other down on that sidewalk. He hadn't wanted to, but he had.

"What if …?" he countered. "We're strangers now. For all I know she's bigamously married and has a dozen kids."

He heard Ellie's sigh through the line. "Glenn … I checked … she isn't, she doesn't. Never married. No kids. If you read the file, you'd know that."

"I read the file." But none of that mattered, he thought. It couldn't. "She'll sign," was all he said, adding, "I'll call you tomorrow. You and Wesley have a good evening."

He doubted he would, but there was no reason for everyone to be miserable.

* * *

Jonah had said casual, and Glenn was glad he'd taken him at his word when he walked through the double doors of the private club. The patrons, as well as the waitstaff, were mostly male.

Glenn paused to let his eyes adjust, taking the moment to let his gaze sweep the room. The furnishings were expensive but unpretentious, the lighting soft but not dim, the voices of the patrons quiet. Probably a place where deals were made, where lives were changed, maybe even destroyed. Colter and Jonah sat at a corner table near the back. Jade wasn't with them, and Glenn let his shoulders relax. He didn't want to have their first, and hopefully last, discussion with an audience.

He watched the two men as he approached their table. The family resemblance was strong. Bellamys, not untouchable but damned near undefeatable. They were deep in conversation, and he had no doubt of the topic. These two weren't simply Jade's work partners, they were her family, and they were her friends. They might or might not think of him as the enemy, but they damned sure wouldn't think of him as either family or friend at this point. He didn't kid himself that they weren't powerful, weren't wealthy. But he wasn't exactly selling apples on a street corner. Hopefully, it wouldn't come to the proverbial pissing contest, but—if it did—he could hold his own.

Jonah saw him first and stood, as did Colter. They shook hands as if they hadn't spent most of the afternoon together, then sat. A waiter approached to take his drink order as Jade's cousins signaled for refills. For some reason, that lessened Glenn's tension. They weren't overly concerned with keeping their wits about them. They were here for conversation, maybe for resolution.

All Glenn wanted was his damned divorce.

Colter was first to wade into the conversation, which surprised Glenn. Although both came across as men of strength, even forces of nature, he'd pegged Jonah as the more aggressive of the two. And maybe aggressive wasn't exactly the right word, but Glenn had no doubt that he could be if and when circumstances warranted that.

"Let's talk about the men who trashed you and hauled you away from ..." Colter stopped and frowned slightly. "Where the hell were you when this happened, anyway? Where was Jade?"

His tone was edgy but Glenn didn't take offense, particularly in light of the fact that Colter hadn't used the phrase 'when you claimed this happened'. That at least was progress.

"A line shack near a place one ranch over from her folks. I'm not sure of the name of the place or the owner. Hilliard, maybe?"

Colter shook his head but Jonah nodded. "Close enough. The Double H. Harp Hillman's place."

Colter snorted. "Blonde and breasts ... that's what you're remembering. You and Harp's oldest daughter had a thing going at the time."

Glenn waited for them to get back on track, which happened fast when Jonah admitted, "Would've kept going if she hadn't been set on settling down right after graduation."

The statement shifted both their gazes back to Glenn, who almost wanted to smile, but he wasn't quite that amused. It had been a mutual desire for him and Jade … at least he'd thought so at the time.

He shrugged, returning the conversation back to the point where they'd been diverted. "Yeah, Hillman sounds right. Anyway, we hadn't quite figured out how to tell Jade's parents we were married. She'd slip away when she could, and I'd be waiting at that old line shack."

Colter frowned. "I guess there were a couple still standing, but they couldn't have been much for shelter."

"I cleaned this one up as best I could. It was enough." In point of fact, the cabin had been sound and sturdy, but the topic, which bordered too close to his memories of holding Jade, body to body, wasn't one he wanted to dwell on with these two men. "Anyway, I hadn't seen Jade in a couple of days. We were supposed to meet the next evening."

"So, when the men came to get you, there weren't any other hands around?"

He met Jonah's gaze, then lowered his to the untouched drink in his hand. "Not up at the line shack. It hadn't been used for years and probably hasn't been since. Besides, it was a Friday after hours. Most wouldn't come in until right at midnight and wake up at sunrise, grouchy with hangovers. They were used to me not going. I wasn't much for getting drunk or groping women I'd never met. In hindsight, maybe I should have, but I doubt it would have made a difference in the end."

He heard the edge in his voice and looked up to find them watching him steadily.

"Jade wanted me gone, and someone made that happen for her."

"You think that's what happened?"

He took a sip of his drink, and set it aside as he let the first swallow burn going down.

"It had to be somebody she'd told … somebody she'd asked to help her. Someone knew where to find me, and when to find me there."

"Not one of the other hands?"

"They knew nothing about Jade. I made damned sure of that. I didn't want her name in their dirty minds and dirtier mouths. They weren't bad or mean or anything, just talked too much trash most of the time."

"So, it was dark that night. You wouldn't be able to identify any of them if we found some old photographs?"

Glenn shook his head. Damned if it didn't sound as if they actually believed him. After a moment he said as much, and Jonah smiled faintly.

"It was your left arm they broke."

Glenn stared at him until he added, "It doesn't straighten all the way when you're relaxed."

"You're pretty damned observant." Most people never noticed that his forearm was slightly crooked. "Even if I could've found a doctor to help me those first few days, I wouldn't have had the money to pay. I'd slept dressed … most of the temporary hands did … so I had my wallet and a little money. The rest of it was hidden in my saddle, in a knife sheath."

He'd missed that saddle, his horse, for a long time, and hoped someone had taken care of him after. He'd stolen food along the way, as often as he could, wherever he could. He never took more than he needed, but he'd been desperate and damned determined to survive.

"So how did you get from a kid with a broken arm and no money to Collier Oil?"

Glenn's smile wasn't intentionally grim, but it was all he could muster. "I busted my ass from 'can to can't', determined to come back and buy or destroy whatever Jade had and whoever she was. By the time I had the means, I no longer cared."

Not quite true, but true enough to count.

Jonah had one last question. "If Jade was so determined to rid herself of you, if she wanted out of the marriage, why are you still married?"

Glenn matched him look for look. "Thinking about it now, if her family really *wasn't* involved, I'd guess she didn't want any of them … any of you … to know she'd lowered herself to marry the likes of me."

Colter studied him a moment before he asked, "So, if she didn't turn to family to rid herself of you, who did she turn to for help?"

Glenn shrugged.

"Seems to me," Colter said, "your theory is as full of holes as Swiss cheese, and I don't much care for either one."

Chapter Twelve

Albuquerque felt soft in the evening light. The lights from storefronts and businesses were dimmed, closed signs hung on glass doors, but beyond the haze, a full moon and stars glittered.

Glenn didn't recall much of the town. There had been a weekend here and there in the time before Jade, when he and some of the others, older than him by a year or two, had drifted down in trucks decades older than they were, to find the beer they weren't legal to have in backstreet places that didn't much care for legalities. Those few experiences hadn't impressed him, and he'd gradually quit going and they'd gradually quit asking.

He'd walked from his hotel to the club and he walked back, declining offers of rides from both men, as he'd declined their offer of an apartment in one of the family-owned complexes. At the moment, there was no ill will between himself and Jade's cousins, and he saw no reason for there to be, but he'd learned not to count on the future. Life was lived in the present and managed a day at a time.

He wasn't accustomed to having to manage either memory or emotion. He'd buried memories of Jade a long time ago, and he kept his emotions in check with logic and reason. Tonight was different. Tonight, memories had surfaced, and anger battled with the questions Jade's cousins had raised. The logic of the kid he'd been didn't mesh with the reasoning of the man he'd become.

His cellphone was ringing as he let himself into his room. He flipped on a few lights and turned toward his unpacked bag. Damn, he hated hotels. He unearthed the phone from his pocket just as it stopped ringing and smiled. Lizbeth. The thought of her, the image it brought to mind made him feel better. She'd been everything good in his life in the last few years.

He immediately pressed the button to return the call.

"Hey, babe." Her voice was immediately soothing. "I was afraid you were out for the evening."

"No," he said huskily. "I'm actually in for the evening. How's my favorite girl?"

She laughed softly. "Missing her favorite guy, that's how."

"I miss you, too," he replied honestly. He wished, in fact, that she was there. She would make everything sane again.

"It's storming here," she said. "Maybe tornadoes tonight, they say. I got soaked getting into my house. What about there?"

The question reminded him that she had no idea where

he was. Or why. Because he wouldn't lie to her, never had, never would, all he said was, "I don't care what the weather does now as long as the sun is shining on the day you become my wife."

She chuckled. "And if it doesn't?"

"Then we'll have to make our own damned sunshine, won't we? But the weather is boring ... tell me about your day."

And she did in her softly funny and entertaining way. He felt like a total jackass for all of the things she didn't know, but he was on a course-correct and, if successful, she'd never have to know or be stressed over things he considered solidly in his past and completely irrelevant to his future. To their future.

* * *

Jade stood staring out the window of her office when she heard the door open behind her. She forced a smile as she turned—only her admin or family entered without knocking.

Colter stepped in and closed the door behind him. "Good morning." He glanced at her desk then back at her. "You read the report?"

She crossed to her desk to get the folder, then motioned toward her small conference table, where she tossed it down, saying, "Yeah, I read it. They caught the guy. I'm glad." She paced the length of her office, then returned to stand behind a chair.

Colter took the chair opposite where she stood. "But you wish it had played out the way we planned it."

"Damn right I do. I was looking forward to getting in a couple of hard punches, maybe a knee to the groin. I wish it even more after reading those reports."

"I wish you'd had that opportunity." He sounded grim. "Those three women had it pretty rough."

She took a deep breath. "The one … have you heard anything else? Is she going to make it?"

"Still critical, but her doctors are hopeful. The other two will be released today. They'll need counseling—they all will—and they'll get it."

"How the hell does a repeat offender hit the streets as often as this guy managed to do?"

"It shouldn't have happened. You know it, and I know it. The previous two offenses were different, lesser," he allowed.

"Not by a hell of a lot." She was still furious … it rolled through her in waves.

"But enough for the judges, apparently."

In the first case, the guy had bound them and fondled himself. He'd been a model prisoner, a shrink's dream, considered rehabilitated and a free man in too few years. The second case, he'd bound them and fondled them. Again, in prison, he'd said and done all the right things, things that helped relieve an overcrowded prison system and work-weary officials. None of which made it right. Not for her.

"He was escalating. They should have seen that."

"They should have," he agreed.

This time he'd raped, and he'd mutilated.

"If they turn him loose again, I'll find him and finish him."

"And I'll help." Colter's voice was as grim as his expression.

At his words, she sighed and finally sank into a chair. "But that's not why you're here."

"It's part of it, but, no, not all of it." He tilted his head. "Do you want to talk?"

"Didn't he?" she countered.

"Some." When she stayed silent, staring him down, he sighed. "Damn it, Jade. What he said doesn't matter nearly as much as what you have to say. Married? What the hell?"

She smiled faintly. "You're not the only person asking that question. I've asked myself that a time or two through the years, but when you're eighteen it isn't about judgement; it's all about the hormones."

"Talk to me," he said softly. "Tell me what happened."

For a moment, she stared at the wall behind him, then shifted her gaze. "I was young, and I thought I was in love. One night we found a preacher and told him I was pregnant, that I needed to be married before I told my folks. Not many weeks later, I went to the cabin where we met as often as I could get there and found a note he'd left for me." She shrugged. "He'd had second thoughts. I was too young. He wasn't ready. He'd come back one day." A deep breath reminded her the pain was still there. "He never did."

"Until now," Colter said.

"Until now."

"Why not file for a divorce, or an annulment, or what the hell ever?"

She shrugged. "At eighteen, I hadn't a clue how to untangle the mess I'd made by getting married. By the time I did know, I didn't give a damn. I knew I'd never trust anyone enough to marry again." She paused before saying softly, "And in all the time between, no one had ever uncovered the fact." At least no one who'd mentioned it to her or to any of the family, especially her brothers, who would have made her life hell over it, or Jonah or Colter, who would've taken her to task but helped her in the end. "After all these years, I couldn't see a reason to create family drama. I knew marriage wasn't for me and never would be." A marriage 'that wasn't' worked fine for me.

"You'll need to talk to him."

"No, I don't. He wants a divorce, after all these years, and I have no reason to oppose that. My attorney can look at his papers and I'll sign anything he thinks is in my best interest."

"After you hear what he has to say," Colter said flatly.

She stared at him. "What the hell, Colter? What is this to you, and why do you care what he has to say?"

"Because you both believe what you're telling me, and I believe both of you even though your stories aren't even close. Someone left a severely beaten eighteen-year-old boy to die and an eighteen-year-old girl with a broken heart. I loved that girl and I love the woman she is now. I'd like to know who made that decision for you, and I'd like to know why."

Jade sat silent, flooded with pain and memories and confusion. Life made a hell of a lot more sense when she was fighting the bad guys.

Glenn's words, his accusations, haunted her. Had there been bad guys she'd never known about?

"What difference can it make at this point?"

"Maybe none as far as your marriage is concerned, but since when have we let the villains twin? Especially where family is concerned."

"You consider him family?"

"Even if I didn't, you are." He sighed. "It may have been long ago, and I may not have known about it until now, but you were hurt and I think it's had a long and hurtful impact on decisions you've made."

"I'm fine," she said stiffly.

"Maybe."

"Damn it, Colter!"

He leaned back in his chair and waited until she gave a huff of resignation. "Fine. I'll talk with him." But God knew she didn't want to.

Seemingly satisfied, Colter shifted the conversation to the neighboring building acquisition and from there to their new forensics division and its new manager.

"I've never seen a man so excited," he said with a smile.

"Robert will do well, and he earned the opportunity to prove it." She smiled back. "And it felt damned good to be the one to tell him that."

Colter got to his feet and studied her a moment. "As much as we love our jobs, they aren't easy, and they aren't always fun."

"Colter, I'm okay," she said, answering the look more than the statement.

After a moment, he nodded and let himself out, and she sat there a little longer, hoping she hadn't lied about that.

When she finally got to her feet, she ignored the work waiting on her desk, unreturned phone calls, unanswered email, and reports. Instead, she walked to the bank of windows and gazed out at the skyline.

She hadn't actually thought about whether or not Glenn had divorced her after he'd abandoned her. She'd assumed it, but it hadn't mattered. The only thing that had mattered was that he had walked away from her, that he hadn't loved her enough to stay.

And she'd never considered remarriage. She'd had flings and she'd had actual lovers, but she'd never, ever let herself fall in love again. She'd never dream of children.

Even now it wasn't too late. More women than not, these days, waited until their late twenties or early thirties to wed and to have their first child. But even now, she couldn't imagine herself doing either. Something inside of her had broken the day Glenn left. Something irreparable.

She'd made a life, and it was a good one. It was, she told herself, all she needed. And even then, something inside of her whispered, what if … what if they had both been betrayed … what if someone had motivation to keep them apart? But who? And why?

And, regardless of who and why, as Colter had asked, since when had the Bellamys ever let the villains win?

Without giving herself more time to think, she went to her computer and dashed off one email to Colter and Jonah and another to her admin and a few other staff, then went to the apartment she called home to pack what little she'd need for the next several days.

Chapter Thirteen

"Where is she?" Glenn asked as Jonah stepped out of the elevator at noon. "All I can get out of whoever the hell is answering her phone is that she's out of the office for a few days."

"I've got a little time. Let's get some lunch."

"I'm not hungry." Damn, he sounded like a petulant bitch.

"Well, I am," Jonah countered as he strode toward the front of the building, "and if you want answers, you'll get them while I eat."

Glenn hesitated, then did the only thing he could do and not look like a jackass.

A host met them at the door to the restaurant on the ground level, glanced from Glenn's face to Jonah, and asked, "Business?"

Jonah nodded. "Family business. Private."

They followed him to a room on one side. It held a single table, five chairs, and a sideboard. "Ring when you're ready," and, with that, the host closed the door behind him.

Glenn schooled himself in patience as Jonah eyed him across the table. He prided himself on being able to read people in a business deal, but this wasn't business, and he couldn't read this man.

"I haven't talked with Jade yet, but Colter did."

Glenn took a deep breath. "And, she'll sign the papers?"

Jonah leaned back in his chair. "She will, but Colter and I agree the two of you need to talk, first."

"What's to talk about?"

"A note signed with your name, telling her you'd made a mistake, weren't ready to settle down, and might come back some day."

Glenn stared at him in momentary confusion, then fury. "That's a damned lie."

"She needs to hear that from you."

"She already knows." The words came from between gritted teeth. "She's the one who created that lie."

Jonah shook his head without anger, and Glenn felt a sickness down deep in his gut.

"She sent an email to me and to Colter late yesterday. Said she was going to the mountain. To think."

"To think or to hide?"

"Hide?" Jonah snorted. "Hell, no. She's running. And, believe me when I tell you, Jade is not a runner."

The girl Glenn had known hadn't been, but Glenn didn't trust anything he'd thought he knew. Not anymore. All he asked was, "Which mountain?"

Jonah watched him with that steady gaze, and Glenn

took a deep breath. He didn't need that answer. He already knew.

* * *

Jade could have borrowed one of the ranch trucks, but she hadn't wanted to see her folks or her brother. Not now. Not when she was this raw. They were too perceptive. There would be too many questions for which she had no answers.

Instead, she'd stopped in a small valley town on the opposite end that catered to out-of-state hunters and rented a dusty but rugged little Jeep. The motor sounded smooth enough to take the mountain road. She wasn't going all the way to the top, but close enough. She slung her duffle in the back along with the few groceries she'd bought. If the cabin still stood, there would still be battered pots and pans as well as the dented coffee pot. Water from the mountain stream was always cool and clear. And she still knew how to build a campfire.

The old dirt road, barely more than a trail now, had her teeth hitting together and her bones feeling like they'd tumbled down a cliff. Worse than the bruising of her body was the battering of her heart as she neared the cabin where she'd left so much of herself behind.

She wasn't sure *why* she was here. She only knew that *here* was where she needed to be. Maybe to sort it all out in her mind. Maybe to ask the questions she hadn't known to ask herself. Maybe to let it go and heal the pieces she'd pretended weren't broken.

Her first glimpse of the cabin caught her off-guard. Her mind had expected deterioration, maybe even to the point of dilapidation. Instead, the old boards, weathered to silver, shimmered in the sunlight, as strong and as solid as the day she'd walked away. She stepped out of the Jeep and breathed mountain air redolent with trees and rock … and memories. For a moment, she let those memories flood her, then she straightened. The past couldn't be recreated, but it could be faced, and she'd do that.

She walked cautiously over the boards of the porch that creaked with her every step. The last thing she needed was a twisted ankle or, God forbid, a broken bone. But the planks held solid as she carried first her duffle and sleeping bag and then the food she'd bought inside. And wine, she reminded herself, don't forget the wine. It probably wouldn't measure up to its full potential out of a tin cup. Better straight from the bottle, but even that prospect didn't faze her.

Maybe she'd drink it all, get drunk and not care, if only for one evening, just not give a damn. About anything.

Once she had everything inside, she pushed the bolt on the door and slid to the rough-plank floor with that bottle of wine, a corkscrew, and a tin cup that she doubted had ever before held liquor of any kind … much less a wine at the top of some sommelier's curated wine list. Exhausted by her own thoughts, by the memories that had chased her mile by mile up the mountain, she let her head drop back against the door behind her and let the memories come.

* * *

The sky was overcast, threatening rain, as her mare picked her way up the slope. Her heart lifted because she knew Glenn waited for her a little farther up the trail. It was the first year her father had allowed her to move on to the next ranch with her brothers for calf branding. Jade knew she wouldn't have been given that permission if the place wasn't their closest neighbor, a couple with daughters of their own. And he damned sure wouldn't have if he'd noticed how often Jade's gaze had followed Glenn as he worked or how often his eyes caught and held hers across the bawling calves they'd been tasked with separating from their mamas.

They wouldn't have long, not that anyone would come looking for either of them. She'd been surprised to discover that the Hillmans tended to let their daughters take care of themselves and treated Jade in the same offhand fashion. If one didn't show up for dinner, the reaction was most often a shrug and 'they'll eat when they're hungry'.

But, while the days were getting longer, darkness fell swiftly when the moon was little more than a sliver. There seemed never enough time to talk and dream with Glenn's arm around her shoulder before he would hustle her down the mountain. But there was now, she thought, as he stepped into the path and took hold of her horse's bridle. There was now, and there was Glenn, and that was all that mattered.

As she slid into his arms, a mist of rain, the barest sprinkle, began to fall.

"Oh, nooo," she said softly, already anxious, already dreading that their time together would be cut short.

"Come see what I found," Glenn whispered in her ear.

She'd go with him anywhere, she thought, anywhere at all.

That was the night the cabin became theirs. That was the night Jade became his.

Afterwards, Glenn rode with her back to the ranch, unsure if they would find house lights on and search lanterns cutting through the dark. They found, instead, a window left open for her by the other girls in a household quietly sleeping.

Glenn held her tight and kissed her again before he gave her a boost to the window sill. She leaned out and watched as he led his horse and hers to the corral, watched as he tossed their saddles onto the railing with the others and turned them loose.

Then he turned back toward the house and she lifted her hand, hoping he could see it in the soft moonlight. She fell asleep dreaming of forever.

* * *

Glenn gave only the briefest thought of calling for his helicopter. Keira could have it at the airport by daylight, and he could be on the mountain, with his bags packed and ready, an hour after that. But the idea of waiting, of spending another night without Jade's signature on what he'd come to consider his release from the past, didn't appeal to him.

Beyond that, the helicopter would be a hell of an announcement to the surrounding ranches. Then he'd still have to make his way from a landing site to the cabin. And he damned sure didn't want an audience of anything more than a herd of doomed but placidly content beef cows watching what happened between him and the girl— woman now—he'd once loved more than life itself, but had come to despise to the depths of his soul.

He wondered if he'd remember the way, if the trees and shrubs had grown and crowded so close he'd miss the turn in the gathering dusk. He wasn't surprised that the horse trail had been widened to accommodate a truck. He was surprised to see lights glowing from the windows. Electricity. The certain bastion of civilization.

For a moment, he sat in the truck, just breathing, pushing back on memories of loss and pain, of broken promises and broken bones. Then, taking a deep breath, he stepped out and walked to the porch.

He didn't knock. He figured the creaking boards had

been enough of an announcement if she was awake. If not, he'd wake her soon enough. He tried to summon some of the anger he'd known through the years, but when he opened the door and stepped inside, all he felt was empty.

Chapter Fourteen

Jade heard the truck motor, had been half expecting it. Maybe more than half. She couldn't imagine a Glenn so changed that he'd wait patiently for her to return. And was that what she'd wanted all along? For him to come to her, to the place where they'd begun … and ended … leaving things unsaid.

She pushed to her feet and braced herself to face him and not run. She hadn't been sure how she'd feel in this moment. They'd been so young, and it had all been so long ago. They'd be little more than strangers now. But when he walked in and fixed his gaze on her, the past seemed suffocatingly close.

"I never thought I'd see you again."

She watched as his jaw clenched, knew he forced

himself to answer, when he said, "I never intended to give you the chance." She hadn't thought his voice would sound so much the same or his eyes would hold the same pull on her senses.

The bewilderment she'd felt all those years ago cascaded through her again. She'd loved him so damned much, had truly believed he loved her. Had believed his words, the touch of his hands and lips, had trusted the passion he'd taught her. Tears burned in her eyes, and she dared them to fall, to expose the hurt that lived forever.

She crossed her arms over her chest and lifted her chin. "You have papers for me to sign, but Colter says you have something to say and I'm to listen to you first."

To her surprise, his lips quirked. "Do you do everything Colter says these days?"

"Almost never," she admitted quietly, then took a deep breath, "but why don't you tell me what he thinks I need to hear, anyway."

Glenn gestured toward the wine bottle. "Do you have another one of those tin cups handy?"

"This is the only one I found, but I'll share…" She filled it and held it out to him.

He took the cup and sank to the floor facing her, close but not too close, crossing his legs in front of him. He took a sip, then another, and then he started talking. "I waited for you that day. Waited for you like I always did. I knew we'd be finished with the Hillman place soon and I wanted us to make plans, to find a way, to take that step, to be together in front of your family and God and everyone." His gaze moved from her to the floor in front of him. "I thought you felt the same, that together we'd figure it out." He cleared his throat. "My guard was down, so maybe it's partly my fault, but there were two of them, so maybe not. They came at me in the dark. My arms were jerked behind my back, and I was blindfolded and gagged. By the time they finished beating me, I was out cold. I woke up to sunshine, a battered body, a broken arm, and an empty highway. The last words I could remember hearing as they used me for a punching bag were that you'd changed your mind and your family was taking care of your problem. Me. I was your problem."

Jade had felt the slow slide of her tears long before he finished. She wanted, desperately wanted, to believe he was lying, because, if true, his words would mean the loss of her family for a betrayal she hadn't deserved. Another part of her, the young girl who had been so in love, wanted to believe that he hadn't willingly left her.

She took a deep breath to steady her voice before she spoke. "You knew my dad, my brothers, worked with them day in and day out and knew their voices."

He shook his head. "They wouldn't bother to take care of their own business, would they? They hired thugs to do it for them."

"That's not the Bellamy way. Not to sneak and not to attack an outnumbered man. Any of them might have, likely would have, come at you face to face, angry at you and disappointed with me, but not like that." She was sure of that. "And they would have come at me first, asked and been sure."

He snorted. "All they had to do was follow us, or someone saw us who went to them."

"I would have known. I promise, I would have known. And, if it were them, sooner or later, they would have arranged an annulment or something, with or without my agreement." She shook her head slowly. "And they wouldn't have left the note here for me to find. They didn't know,

Glenn. They still don't know."

She could tell he didn't agree, but Glenn didn't know her family. She did. Getting to her feet, she picked up her duffle and dumped the contents onto the bed before unzipping the tiny side pocket near the bottom. She stared at the folded scrap of paper before carrying it back across the room and handing it to Glenn.

She didn't have to read it again, that scrap of paper softened over the years by much handling. The words never left her, hadn't since the day he'd left.

He read the note and seemed to read it again, then he looked at her and said, "Fuck."

It wasn't a word she cared for or used, but she couldn't call it inappropriate, not at the moment. She wanted to cry, but she didn't. She wanted to curse, but she didn't. Neither tears nor words, however ugly, would undo the damage that had been done.

* * *

Glenn woke on a hard floor beneath him, a warm blanket over him, and a headache. They'd passed that lone cup back and forth between them until Jade had poured the last drop from the bottle, offering it to him … and he'd needed it, taken it.

Across the small room, Jade lay curled inside a sleeping bag. Moonlight through the unshuttered windows teased the lighter tones from her hair. Hair that most people thought black at a glance. She'd fallen asleep before him, and when her restless shifting had quieted, he'd fallen asleep as well. But, he realized, she'd awakened at some point and eased the blanket over his shoulders.

With quiet movements, he got up and stepped outside.

The clean mountain air held the chill he remembered from so long ago. He took a deep breath, needing to sort through all of the thoughts twisting through his brain. Nothing seemed to be as he'd been so completely convinced it was. Now the *what ifs* tormented him. What if he'd turned around and walked right back across that state line to find her, to face her? What if he'd come back in the early years when she'd still haunted him, before he'd pushed thoughts of her to that small space inside his mind that she'd never truly left. The hell of it was, it was too late, and he'd never know. And now there was Lizbeth.

He'd been tempted to step back into the truck and return the way he'd come. Almost. But there was unfinished business and signing divorce papers now seemed the least of it. He wasn't a kid anymore, and the man he'd become wanted answers. And, maybe, vengeance as well.

He let his gaze sweep the mountains around him. He'd seen a lot of incredible places through the years, but the mountains of New Mexico tugged at him in ways other places never had. He turned to go back inside, when a sweep of wings turned his gaze upward to an outcropping of rocks, silver in the light from the moon. A quick flash of déjà vu stopped him in place. The dream again. The body, already stiffened by death, tumbling down, almost end over end in a macabre descent. A feeling of someone watching from above, but when he turned to look, there was no one.

Shaking it off, he went back into the cabin and sat with his back against the wall, watching Jade sleep. As a young girl she'd been pretty, sun-browned and lithe, with a sharp mind and quick wit. The woman in front of him wasn't beautiful, at least not classically so—not like Lizbeth whose perfect features graced countless pages and screens, her body almost fragile. Jade's features were strong and stunning, her curves built for a man to hold.

He hadn't let himself think of her much in the years since—even after the anger had burned out. There had been times, he admitted now, moments when a girl's laughter rang out, when a young couple about the age they'd been walked by hand in hand, when the autumn air turned crisp and chill—especially then—she would cross his mind briefly. But he never let himself dwell in that place, never let himself wish, never even let himself grow bitter.

He'd built a life for himself. A good life. But knowing, hell, accepting, that it had all been ripped away, not just from him, but from the both of them, scattered ashes he thought he'd buried long ago.

As the wood creatures stirred to life around the cabin, the sounds of birds calling and squirrels chattering, Jade roused as well. When she sat, she didn't look away as he'd expected her to do, she didn't try to straighten her hair or rub the sleep from her eyes. She took a deep breath, and her lips curved in a faint smile.

"I won't ask if you slept well."

He chuckled, and that surprised him as much as her smile. "Best not."

The smile faded. "What now?"

He almost answered the question as simply as she'd asked it, but that moment of déjà vu had stirred other thoughts than a signature on divorce papers. "I need to find out whose body I saw pushed from a cliff a night or two before I was beaten and left for dead."

Jade's color faded, and he cursed himself as he recalled how her brother had died. But Silas had been caught in that rockslide long after he was gone. Glenn would never even have known if he hadn't read the information Ellie had gathered. Still, for Jade it had to be a deep wound that never healed.

But he'd felt something, hadn't he? A thought, a brush of hidden memory as he'd read through those files. It had to have been this memory of a body tumbling, gaining speed, and hitting hard against rock and dirt. Had there been shadowy figures or only shadows? Or maybe all of it no more than a dream.

In any case, he had to know for sure.

He looked at Jade who had wrapped her arms around her knees and lowered her head. "I'm sorry, babe. I know about Silas—his accident—but this memory I have, whatever it is, isn't like that."

Jade lifted her head, met his gaze, and his words slammed back at him. The endearment had come effortlessly, but that, too, was nothing more than a relic of times past, a love past.

She didn't comment, just stood and began gathering the bedroll. When she finished, he took it from her and carried it to the Jeep, then came back and waited as she stuffed her scattered belongings into the duffle.

He picked up the blanket and rolled it into a ball. "Thanks for this," he said.

She hesitated, then shrugged. "I couldn't let you freeze to death, but there was a time I wished you dead."

He nodded. "Fair enough."

"I guess you felt the same about me."

He almost didn't answer, but when he did it was honestly. "No, not dead. I wanted to hate you. I wanted you to be alive and miserable."

As he had been. The thought hung between them as he followed her out the door.

* * *

Jade glanced in her rearview occasionally. Just, she told herself, to be sure Glenn was managing the mountain road without difficulty. It had been a while since he'd been on these mountains. They could be treacherous. Besides, when he had, it had been sure-footed mountain horses who took as good care of their riders as they did themselves.

She still had no idea how she felt, a realization that was as unfamiliar as it was unsettling. It should have been easy to reel her thoughts in, but they were scattered far and wide. Accepting that, she did what Bellamys do best, she focused on the concrete. Someone, presumably a man, had died and Glenn had witnessed whatever it was that happened. A day or two, or a few, later he'd been railroaded out of town. Glenn, she felt sure, had not yet put those pieces together. But his job was drilling for oil hundreds, even thousands of feet below the ocean floor. Hers was connecting the dots and finding justice for the dead and the surviving. Which was why she hit Colter's name on her cell phone as soon as the signal was strong enough to hold a real conversation.

Chapter Fifteen

They were halfway down the mountain when Glenn's phone rang. He glanced at the name and lifted a brow. Colter Bellamy. Interesting. He hit the speaker button and answered, not rudely, but neither with a great deal of welcome.

Colter didn't seem to mind. "I'd like for you to check out of your hotel. We'll have an apartment ready before you get back, including a liquor cabinet and stocked refrigerator. What's your beer?"

"I planned to check out but didn't really plan on sticking around. I have the divorce agreement. Short and sweet and it won't take Jade long to read and sign."

"I'll message the entrance address for the parking garage. Security has your name and a parking place assigned.

Jade's apartment is on the floor above yours. Company-owned building. There's plenty of small conference rooms scattered around if you need one, because we may have a bigger problem than getting the two of you unhitched. See you soon." And, before Glenn could answer, he disconnected.

Glenn wavered between frustration and amusement. The Bellamys were a bossy bunch. Maybe it was a good thing he hadn't been around for his marriage.

Besides, he was fairly bossy himself; it came with the territory. He didn't mind checking out of his suite. Luxury though it was, hotels were not his favorite. He had no doubt a Bellamy-provided apartment would beat anything else in the city. Whether or not he'd stay more than the time it took for Jade to read the divorce agreement and voice any concern was debatable.

And at least there would be alcohol. He'd likely need it before this was done. He'd worry about that 'bigger problem' when he got there.

* * *

It didn't take long for Glenn to gather his belongings and check out, assuring the manager on duty that everything had been to his liking and that his leaving was business related. Not exactly true but not too far off the mark, he told himself. Business, yes, but personal.

When he pulled into the parking garage at the address he'd been given, he wasn't surprised to find it enclosed, temperature controlled, and brightly lit. The guard was initially cautious but immediately welcoming when Glenn showed his identification. He was given a pass key that he was assured would open elevator doors as well as the door to the apartment he'd been given. He parked in the space near the elevator as he'd been told and climbed out.

For a moment, Glenn stood looking at his duffle and briefcase in the back seat and then pulled them out. Faster to bring both down with him if he decided to leave than it would be to come back to retrieve them. If he chose to stay.

He noticed the elevator had a door on either side, so when he stepped out on the fourth floor, he wasn't surprised to find his opened directly into what appeared to be a foyer. Nor was he surprised to find Jade's cousins waiting for him.

Dropping his duffle and briefcase near the door, he stepped forward, shaking the hand each held out to him. He took one of the empty chairs and Jonah handed him a bottle and an opener. After glancing at the label in appreciation, Glenn pulled the cap and leaned back in his chair, glancing from one to the other.

Colter shrugged. "Jade's place is one floor up. She'll be here in," he glanced at his watch, "five."

Glenn suspected it was closer to ten before she let herself in, but the beer was good and he was in no hurry. Curious about that 'bigger' problem they were to discuss, but not stressed.

Her glance met his, and he felt a pull he'd moved past long ago. Or so he'd thought. She looked at the bottles in their hands then walked to the sideboard and poured a glass of wine from a bottle that had been opened but was still full. Glenn felt certain her cousins knew her preference.

When she returned to the table she took the only chair left, the one opposite him. Only in the moment that Jonah and Colter both turned their gazes to her did Glenn realize this meeting was at her instigation. He sat straighter and placed his beer on the table, not tense but not as relaxed as he'd been a moment before.

His gaze went straight to her. "So, what is this bigger problem we have?" he asked, quoting Colter.

She didn't miss a beat. "Bigger than what?"

"Bigger than getting us unhitched, according to your cousin." He didn't bother clarifying which one.

"Tell them about the body you saw falling."

For an instant he felt like that kid with his arms tied behind his back, while he was used as a punching bag. "What the hell, Jade. Is this some kind of scare tactic? You haven't even seen the damned divorce papers."

Jonah caught on quicker than Jade. "Get a grip, cowboy, this isn't a shakedown."

Glenn watched as shock, then fury, then hurt flashed across Jade's face. Even then, she said nothing, just watched him.

That flash of hurt had his muscles untensing. "Sorry," he said finally, then looking at her, not her cousins, he repeated, "I'm sorry, Jade."

She nodded, slowly, and he turned his gaze toward Jonah. "I'm not even sure that what I remember is real. I'm half convinced I dreamed it or hallucinated. Hell, I don't know."

"Tell us anyway."

So, he did, knowing how unrealistic it sounded. The moonlight. The body stiff with rigor-mortis. The slow, sickening tumble. He watched Jade as he talked, thinking of her brother buried under a pile of rocks. It was not the same, but still, he hated to keep bringing up old memories.

"And how long after that were you beaten and dragged out of state?"

He frowned and turned to Colter, still half caught in

the macabre memory and half worried about the impact of his words on Jade. He shrugged. "Honestly, I'm not entirely sure. I think only a day, but it could have been two. And I'm serious when I say I've never been completely sure I saw that body falling … that I didn't dream the whole thing."

"I don't believe in coincidences," Jonah said. "Never have, never will."

"Jade's folks didn't know about your marriage, didn't pay some asshole to beat you to a pulp and dump your body, which is what I suspect those guys thought they'd done."

Glenn shook his head at Colter's words. "How do you know? How can you be sure?"

"I asked," Colter said simply. "They had no clue what I was talking about. No clue that Jade was married, much less at eighteen."

Jade drew a sharp breath, pulling Glenn's focus to her. She hadn't known then about the conversation her cousin had just revealed, hadn't known that her parents now knew about her marriage, knew that at eighteen years old their daughter had been married with no husband around. Interesting family, this one, he thought.

"Think about the timing, Glenn," Colter pressed. "You saw what you shouldn't have and someone caught a glimpse of you. Maybe more than a glimpse. They watched a day, maybe two, before they made a move. You were a sitting duck in that cabin."

Glenn thought about it, and he watched Jade as he did so. Her face was pale, and she bit her lip so hard, he expected blood to drip.

Damn it, they'd been kids. Kids in love, or thinking themselves in love and a little stupid, but they hadn't deserved what had happened to them.

He nodded at Colter and said, "Go on," but it was Jonah who picked up with the answer.

"You're good at what you do, Collier. I've done my homework. Your name stands out in the oil industry. But we're every bit as good at what we do. Pulling threads together, seeing patterns, matching the pieces of a puzzle to ensure an arrest and a conviction."

Glenn thought about that. "So, you believe I had the hell beat out of me not because I married a Bellamy daughter, but because I saw someone disposing of a body. Maybe a murder victim."

Jonah answered with a blunt, "Yes. That's exactly what we think."

Yeah, Glenn thought, he knew oil rigs. He also knew when he was out of his league in something. And he saw their surprise when he asked, "So, what's next?"

Jonah turned to Colter who explained, "We'd like you to work with an expert who will document your memories, maybe pull some things that you don't remember."

"No hypnosis." Glenn didn't trust anyone that much.

Colter grinned. "Don't blame you there, but that's not what we're suggesting. We've got someone on retainer who's really good at asking the right questions. We stole her from the local PD and she has her own practice now, making them pay her big bucks for her services."

"You don't have to commit, up front," Jonah added. "We're asking you to talk with her and let her explain how she works."

Glenn looked at Jade, who was watching him steadily. Once upon a time, he could read her every thought. Not now. She'd learned to keep her feelings shuttered, as he had. She'd sign those papers, he thought. He could be on his way home, back to the Keys, in the morning.

And whoever had damaged the kids they'd been, destroyed the life they'd planned … maybe to cover a crime, maybe for the hell of it … would forever get away with what they'd done.

Slowly, he nodded. "I'll talk with her."

"I'll set it up for in the morning." Colter stood and Jonah followed suit. "We both plan to stay in the city until we get a handle on this, but we'll get out of your hair for now. There are several really good restaurants nearby and the city streets are safe to walk, but there's also one on the top level with a nice menu, and they provide room service if you'd rather."

Jade stayed in her chair while Glenn walked them to the door. Neither glanced back at her which made him wonder if this was pre-planned. And why. He returned to the table and sat. After a minute, her expression eased. "I guess we could play twenty questions."

"You go first," he said, feeling faint traces of a heartache that was sixteen years old, wondering if she did as well.

"Are you happy?"

"Mostly. You?"

"Mostly," her lips curved faintly as she parroted him. "You're engaged."

He supposed one of the cousins told her. "It seemed to be time."

She tilted her head at that. "Time? Like an appointment that must be kept?"

Damn, he thought, as he shook his head. "More than that." But hell if it didn't sound emotionless when put like that. Maybe it wasn't the fire and joy he'd felt with Jade, but it wasn't without emotion.

Thankfully, she moved on. "I'm glad for you."

"Now that you no longer wish me dead?"

She smiled sadly. "I guess it was more that I wished I could wish you dead. It all hurt so much, Glenn."

On impulse, he stood and held out his hand to her. "Let's take a walk and find a place to eat, maybe catch up a little before I have to give myself over to an inquisition in the morning. I think you know far more about me than I do you."

She looked up at him in hesitation. "Why? What's the point of knowing? Who hurt you, I get. We need to know who, maybe even why, but more than that?" She shrugged.

Hand still open, he smiled. "Because we loved, we cared, and, I think, both of us still care." And maybe still loved, although their story was done. The thought wasn't a comfortable one, but Glenn had never shied away from discomfort of any kind.

She placed her hand in his and let him tug her to her feet. "I don't eat fish."

"I remember." Jade found the process of picking around the tiny bones tedious. He remembered that and a lot of other things. Too many.

As they stepped into the elevator, he tried not to think of those other things.

Chapter Sixteen

As they fell into step, Jade glanced up at the moon. It was almost full and brighter than the lights from the storefronts closed for the evening. As much as she loved the ranch, she'd discovered she loved this city more. It was old and imperfect, but its people were warm and friendly. Not all, no, but every city had its share of the good, the bad, and even the evil.

"Tell me how you got into the oil business."

He grunted, but when she turned to look at him, she caught his smile. "The hard way, of course. I worked whatever job came my way ... usually the hard ones because kids eat last at every table. But in a year or two I wasn't the youngest or the scrawniest, and I damned sure wasn't the laziest. I kept walking and working, heading south slowly but surely."

"Why south?"

She was curious but immediately sorry she asked when he said, "No mountains, no memories, nothing but Texas flatlands and, eventually, the gulf. I ended up as cheap labor on an oil rig but I outworked everyone around me and got picked up by a crew and a boss who saw potential, and maybe something else."

"So, he mentored you," she said softly.

"I suppose that's what you could call it. He fed me and kept me alive, but he also taught me and never cut me any slack so I learned not to cut myself any, either."

A self-made man, she mused to herself, careful not to say it aloud. He'd been forced to grow to manhood in the harshest of conditions, and he'd thought her the reason for that, all these years.

"And now you're Collier Oil. You did more than survive, Glenn; you created your own world."

"And what did you do while I was blistering in the sun and saltwater winds?"

Before she could answer, she saw a sign ahead. "Let's eat there. They have the best pasta."

Glenn raised his brow at the sign. "Italian? In Albuquerque?"

"Yes, come on!" She grabbed his hand and tugged, an action she regretted the instant she realized what she'd done.

He moved with her, but his fingers didn't close around hers as they once would have. Nor did she want them to, and she released his hand as soon as he turned with her toward the entrance.

She regretted her choice, as well, when they walked through the door and the dusky lighting closed around them, dimmer even than the afterhours storefront lighting they'd walked under to get here. It was an intimate setting. A setting for lovers. Which they would never be again. Neither of them wanted that, of course, but the memories were still haunting, still painful.

Glenn didn't seem to notice, however, and after a moment she relaxed as Glenn spoke quietly to the host and they waited to be seated. They were fortunate that it was early evening on a weekday. The after-work diners were leaving, and the late-night diners were not yet in full force.

As they read the menus placed before them, a server brought a bottle of wine for Glenn's approval. Jade glanced at the label, recognizing it as the one she'd chosen earlier. She wasn't surprised he'd noticed. She supposed he was used to dating women who expected that of him. But those kinds of touches weren't part of her expectations—weren't anything she wanted or needed. She accepted a business dinner or girls' night out invitation here and there but not romantic ones.

After their server had poured the wine and a waiter had taken their order, Glenn returned to the question she hadn't answered.

"You only ever wanted to be a cowgirl," he reminded her. "Now you're a badass detective."

She smiled. "I prefer badass investigator."

"Is there a difference?"

"Not really. The licensing, educational, and experience requirements are about the same for either in most states."

"Do you still ride?"

"I do, not as often as I'd like, but I try to take a weekend here and there. It's my way to de-stress."

Not until their server brought their salads, and she had to sit back did she realize how close she was leaning toward him.

She stayed slightly further back as she picked up her fork. "What about you, still ride?"

"I have a couple of horses," he said with a shrug, "but not much time to ride them. The oil business is good, better than, but there's always something that needs attention."

"And you're a hands-on kind of boss, I'd guess … but I never pictured you on the water," she said, then bit her lip at what that revealed … not to him as much as to herself. All these years, she'd convinced herself he was far from her mind.

He smiled wryly. "And I would never have pictured you in the city."

Not trusting herself to follow this chain of thought to a comparison of what was to what could have been, she said, "Tell me about your fiancée. How did you meet?"

"At a fund-raising event … she was a friend of a friend of a friend kind of thing. We've been together a while."

And that said volumes about him and his engagement. Or, she told herself, maybe it didn't.

They didn't rush over dinner but neither did they linger. She was almost surprised when they stepped out onto the sidewalk afterward and he didn't turn back the way they'd come.

"Did you ever want to do or be anything except climb your way up the company ladder?"

"Most people assume I had an elevator to the top."

"You don't sound bitter about that assumption."

She shrugged. "Bitterness, like frustration, is a waste of energy."

"Is that how you feel about all emotions now?"

She stopped, and they faced each other. "No, what happened didn't shut me down, but it taught me to treasure the good things. Not right away, but eventually. Happiness and joy and contentment, those are worth something. Even anger, if it pushes you to do something constructive. Bitterness is anger turned inward and destructive. I don't have time for that."

"And I don't make assumptions," he said, "and, while we didn't know each other long, I think I knew you well. I never felt you expected things to be handed to you. You were gritty and determined, and I don't recall a damned time you didn't fight to get a roped calf secured because that meant the calf's safety." He laughed softly, adding, "And you didn't want help because someone might think you weren't as tough as the guys."

Because his words stirred memories better left in the past, she didn't acknowledge them with anything more than a faint smile as she turned and started walking again. "Well, I can't claim that I got my start in the mailroom, but I did earn my way. It wasn't easy, but it was fun all the same."

"Is it still?"

"Fun?" She thought about that before answering. "Sometimes, maybe mostly, but not all. Sometimes the bad guys win. Sometimes innocent people die."

Her tone had turned pensive, and Glenn knew there were things that kept her from sleep at night. In some ways it was hard to match this tough, capable woman with the girl he'd married. In other ways, they were one and the same.

They talked of other things, impersonal things like politics and world events, until they parted ways when he stepped out of the elevator. He glanced back to find her watching him as the doors slid closed.

He walked to the sidebar and poured himself a shot of whiskey. Glancing around the room filled with comfortable furnishings, he went to stand at the window with its view of the street in front of the parking garage. An empty street, he thought, although it was one of the busiest sections of town by day.

As he started to turn away, a barely noticeable movement caught his attention. Stepping back, he switched off the lamp, then returned to the window, letting his eyes adjust to the dark. Several minutes passed before he made the outline of the figure standing against the wall of the opposite building. Another few passed before the figure moved, walking to the edge of the sidewalk and staring up.

Easing back, he called Colter, who answered on the first ring with, "Problem?"

"Maybe, does your apartment face front or back?"

"Front."

"Don't get caught, but step to the window and look across the street."

"As you speak," Colter returned. Then, "Damn."

"I think it's better if whoever that is doesn't know he's been seen. No need to get him replaced by someone sharper."

"Agree. I'll let Jonah know. Could be nothing."

Could be, but Glenn was betting it was something. He wasn't ready to bet on what that something might be, but he didn't believe in coincidence or chance any more than he believed in unicorns or the tooth fairy.

Chapter Seventeen

They gathered in a spacious room two floors up, not quite an office, not quite a meeting room. It held a fully stocked bar, a conference table, and a lounging area with an oversized desk in one corner.

Samantha Everleigh was the last thing he'd expected. He placed her age between forty-five and fifty. With her diminutive stature and easy grin, she looked more like a leprechaun than a professional at whatever she was trained to be. Glenn still wasn't sure what that was. There was no title, no PhD on her uniform. Hell, it wasn't even a uniform, or at least not much of one. Black button-up shirt. Black denim jeans. Blue eyes danced with humor and a hint of mischief, dark hair threaded with traces of silver, pulled up and knotted on top of her head.

She took one look at his face and laughed. "Relax. I'm neither a dentist nor a doctor and I've no needle or other sharp instrument to poke at you or into you."

"But you are Irish," he retorted, "and maybe a little fey."

Samantha gave him a broad smile. "You've been to Ireland, then."

"I have, and I loved it, and hope to go again."

"Are the Irish that easily identified?"

"Maybe not all of you."

"But me," she persisted. "I am?"

"You are," he retorted.

That seemed to please her as she pulled a notebook and pen from her briefcase and looked from Jade and her cousins back to Glenn. "Ignore all of these other people and choose a comfortable-for-you place to sit."

He gave her a quick glance as she seemed to understand that deep, cushy chairs were not his preference, were not where he could relax.

When she chose the desk, placing her notebook on the surface, he pulled a side chair from against the wall. He turned it opposite the desk, then straddled it, crossing his arms over the chair's back.

"No recorder?" he asked.

She shook her head. "I find them distracting, and I suspect many of my clients do as well. Besides," she flashed him a smile, "I don't need them."

Pulling her notebook close, she flipped it open and took up her pen. "I know from Colter that there's a memory from your past that has gaps. Your brain is giving you bits and pieces of an episode in time, but is holding back others."

She paused long enough for him to insert a question if

he had one, which he did. "Intentionally?"

"Maybe, or maybe they've been crowded to a corner by things that happened after … usually shortly after, but not always. Regardless of why you don't remember, those pieces are still there. If you want those gaps closed, we'll find those bits. Tell me what you can't remember by telling me what you can. I'm ready when you are," she finished simply.

For a moment, Glenn wasn't sure where to start. He closed his eyes and waited a few minutes, gathering his thoughts, what memories he *did* have. "It was half light, with the sun sinking below the horizon. Still casting light enough to see but the shadows were getting deeper."

"Where were you?"

"On the mountain."

"What mountain?"

He started to speak, faltered. Hell, he didn't *know* what mountain. He could take her there easily but, if he'd ever known the name, he didn't know it now. He turned toward Jade. "I was headed to the cabin from the Hillman place."

"It likely has a formal name, but we always called it Easy Ridge," she said quietly.

Samantha raised a brow. "Why Easy?"

Jade shrugged. "Because it's anything but that."

She nodded, then turned her attention back to Glenn. "Which side of the mountain?"

"The Hillman's." He was sure of that. He wasn't sure of much else, but being certain of anything was reassuring. He'd just left the Double H headed to the mountaintop, to Jade.

That memory hadn't faded. His thoughts, his feelings, those were the things that punched him in the gut.

"Were you going up the ridge or down?"

"Up from the Hillman's." The cabin was slightly downslope after the peak. He frowned as bits and pieces of memory seeped back in. "There was lightning, and a chill wind. It carried the smell of the rain that hadn't yet arrived."

"The lightning … close enough to hear the crack of it, or was it a rumble still?"

"Too close … enough to make me flinch, tough guy that I was at eighteen." Until three men proved him wrong. And there, he discovered, was a piece he hadn't known was missing. In his mind, he'd only ever recalled two men busting into that cabin. There had been a third, standing in a dark corner, watching and not getting his hands dirty or bloodied.

"For a moment, picture yourself at the base of the mountain, walking up. What would you see in those flashes of light?"

"Packed dirt, scattered rock in all sizes, tufts of grass no good for grazing."

"Further up?"

"Even less grass up the mountain. It gets the harshest wind from the north."

"What would you see if you were on the other side?"

"Softer landscape but not by a whole lot. There are some streams that feed small valleys so the grass grows. Rocks are bigger, more like boulders."

"So, back on the Hillman side, near the top?"

"Near the top is where the going gets tough. You want to pay attention if you hear anyone above you. The rocks are bigger there but more easily unseated because the ground stays softer around some of those streams. And there are trees … pine. I don't know the name. Most of the hands, me included, called all pines a piñon, no matter what they look like."

"What was the lightning like near the top on that night?"

"Like hell broke loose. The streaks were wide, cutting through the clouds, and lighting up whole areas." He paused, frowned. "Then the light changed."

"The lightning changed?"

"Not lightning. There were headlights … just the headlights shining into space." He stopped for a moment, then murmured. "That's where I saw the body, then."

Until he opened them, he didn't realize he'd closed his eyes in concentration as the scene changed. The others stared at him with varying expressions, from stunned to intrigued, but none of them doubtful.

"Body?" Samantha's question, asked softly, still cut through the silence.

Glenn took a breath and nodded. "Through the years, sometimes I've thought it a nightmare. Sometimes, it felt like a memory I could never quite grasp. It was real." He was sure now. "The body was already stiff, and it was shoved from an outcropping of rock. It fell end over end, then bounced in places on the way down."

"Was the fall from above you?"

He met Jonah's steady gaze. "Not directly above. A couple hundred feet up but to the right of where I stood."

"Could whoever was there have seen you?"

"Maybe while I watched it falling. When I looked up again, the headlights were receding."

"You never told me any of this," Jade said without inflection. A glance at her expression convinced him she wasn't making an accusation, simply stating a fact.

"I think you didn't come that night." He hesitated. "And maybe I was gone the next."

"And, maybe," Colter said, "we now know why."

Glenn turned his attention to Samantha. "How did you do all of this? Are you a good witch or a bad witch?"

The woman didn't bristle at what could have been taken as an insult, although Glenn's inflection was anything but. Instead, she laughed. "Neither. Nor am I a magician or a hypnotist. Experts—also which I am not—say that sometimes people don't know what they remember until someone asks a question that sparks it."

"But you know what to ask," Glenn countered.

"Not always. Mostly, I know how to listen. The very fact that someone is listening intently and with purpose can be enough to clear the way for a breakthrough. And, by the way, I'm not Irish, either. I'm Basque."

"Well, hell," Glenn said with wry good humor. "I got it wrong all the way around."

"I helped a little with that," Samantha admitted with a smile. "But the memory you got right." She hesitated, then added, "But it may still not be complete. Memory is an area where our minds can play tricks on us, and those tricks can be used against us by others."

She stood, shifting her attention from him to the others. "And, with this kind of revelation, I suspect you all have business to discuss. If you need me again, you know how to reach me."

At the door, she paused and turned back. "I may not need to say this, Glenn, but I will. You now have knowledge that someone thinks is still hidden. Someone with every reason to want to keep it hidden. You need to be extremely cautious with that knowledge until you know more."

* * *

Not until the door closed behind her, did Glenn turn

toward Jade. "It may be too late for caution."

With a sense of foreboding, Jade knew, already knew, what he was going to say. So, she said it for him. "I know who died."

Glenn exhaled. "I know where the body is buried."

Colter glared from one to the other. "What do Cargill's blackmail notes have to do with this?"

"Apparently, not only Cargill's." Jonah's drawl held more than a touch of irritation as he pinned Jade with a look. "Am I wrong?"

"No, you're not wrong, Jonah." But her gaze stayed on Glenn. "But all of this … what you saw that night … the notes it seems we both got … those aren't what brought you here. It was the divorce?"

"I've never believed in quirks of fate," he admitted, "but damned if this isn't one."

"Whoever sent the notes won't see it that way." Colter's voice was grim.

Jonah nodded agreement. "You're both in danger until this is resolved."

"But who is Cargill?" Glenn asked. "And how the hell does he fit in?"

It was Jade who answered. "Cargill is a local business man … Director of City Council Services. It's not an elected position, but he has political aspirations, at least on a city level. He started as an attorney and most of his associates view him as above average and fairly decent in his dealings. As for how he fits in, I have no idea. He passed along two blackmail notes, asking for my help in finding out who sent them and why."

Glenn frowned. "Does he know you received the same notes?"

Jade grimaced as her cousins glowered. "Until today,

until *now*, no one knew."

"And I'm sure you have a damned good reason why that is," Colter commented.

She winced at Colter's sarcasm, but she couldn't fault him for it. Her only response was, "It seemed a good idea at the time."

* * *

Jade didn't dream of bodies tumbling through a night filled with lightning flashes. She dreamed of bare feet splashing through a shallow stream and wildflowers scattered across valleys and peeking from rocks as if tucked away there by mountain fairies.

She dreamed of Glenn holding her hand as they ran laughing for the sheer joy of it. Of her longing to be his, completely and in every way. It was impractical, impossible, her parents would never let her marry so young. She knew all of those things, but she wouldn't let go of her dream, also knowing that, in the end, they'd forgive and support her. She also knew she'd never want anyone as much as she wanted Glenn. And she'd been right. She never had.

She woke to daylight streaming through cracks in the drapes and tears sliding from the corners of her eyes.

A shower helped, a little makeup helped, but neither vanquished the overwhelming sadness she felt. For years, decades even, she'd had her anger toward Glenn, toward being abandoned, to bolster her. Now there was nothing left except sorrow and regret.

Chapter Eighteen

Glenn didn't dream at all and didn't even sleep until sometime after midnight. He showered, opened his laptop, and opened the latest financial reports for Collier Oil. The recently repaired rig was functioning at full capacity. Sales for the past 30 days trended steadily, neither rising nor falling outside forecast parameters. He reviewed and approved the hiring of an additional instrumentation technician on one rig and the conditional suspension of a drilling engineer on another. That suspension would become termination if the employee failed to complete an inpatient alcohol recovery program.

Logging out of the company database, he opened his personal email and read a long letter from Lizbeth filled with photographs of venues from Central Park to

Hermitage Bay, lists of caterers, and thoughts on music and vows. He closed his eyes, but all he could see was Jade.

* * *

It was mid-morning when he found his way to a room on an upper floor of the Bellamy Building. Colter faced a slowly-lowering projection screen across the room from where he sat with an open laptop in front of him. He glanced up as Glenn walked in and gestured toward the back of the room. "There's coffee and whatever."

Glenn had already had more than enough coffee; even so, he poured himself another cup and carried it to a chair on one side of the U-shaped table arrangement. Jonah walked in a few minutes later, whistling, and Jade not long after.

Her suit, no doubt, was a designer label. The tiny studs in her ears, Tiffany or Cartier. He liked her a damned sight better in scuffed boots and faded jeans. Her scowl looked like the beginning of an argument.

Her gaze swept the room, then moved from Jonah to Colter. She took a deep breath. "Thank you. I know neither of you agree with me about how I handled the notes."

Not the beginning—Glenn quickly changed his assumption—the reopening of an ongoing dispute.

"It's far from settled," Jonah said firmly.

Colter nodded agreement, adding, "But we're willing to discuss."

Jade's chin lifted, and Glenn caught a glimpse of the stubborn girl he remembered.

"Discuss all you want, but this is going to be handled like any other case ... between the three of us and whatever support we collectively decide to bring in. This is who we are and what we do and we do it damned well." She took a breath. "You both know if Uncle Marcus or Uncle Reggie get involved, they'll involve my dad. If that happens, I'll strike out on my own and not a one of you will know where I am or what I'm up to."

Glenn managed not to laugh at their expressions.

Ignoring their reaction to her threat, she walked to the sideboard and loaded a plate with croissants, fruit and pastries before dropping her briefcase on the floor and taking a chair opposite Glenn. Their eyes met, and when she saw his grin, she smiled faintly and relaxed against the back of her chair.

"I'll make one amendment to Jade's edict," he commented. "This will be handled by the *four* of us. Detective work may not be my vocation, but I'm damned good at finding answers and unearthing secrets. Besides, which, I have a vested interest ... my own pair of blackmail notes."

He was watching Jade more than her cousins, saw when she winced and closed her eyes briefly before opening her briefcase. He kept his gaze on her as she pulled a plastic sleeve with a single piece of paper. "Make that three."

She passed the sleeve to Glenn, first. He read it before handing it to Colter, but the words stayed with him, as terse and as easily remembered as the first two. 'A million buys my silence'.

Pulling his phone from his pocket, he pushed back his chair and got to his feet, pacing the length of the room until Ellie answered.

"Good morning. Are you headed back? Papers signed?"

"Not exactly."

Silence. Then, "That's the answer you gave me the last time I asked."

"It's complicated."

"What can I do to uncomplicate it?"

And that, he thought, that air of readiness and calm confidence, was why he kept her on retainer. "I need you or someone you trust to bring some things from the safe in my home office to Albuquerque."

Again, she didn't hesitate. "That won't be a problem."

"And any envelope the cleaning service has placed on my desk that doesn't have a return address."

When she spoke again her tone had changed, proving she recognized a threat of some kind. "I've always wanted to see New Mexico. What is it you want from your safe?"

"Two plain white envelopes, both addressed to me, but neither has a return address."

"I'll get my travel agent on the phone while I pack an overnight."

"Don't bother. I'll send the jet to pick you up in the Keys when you let me know the timing. Give the pilot your car keys so I can have it moved to St. Pete. That way you can fly straight home … after you and Wesley take a vacation on me. Bring more than an overnight bag. New Mexico is beautiful this time of year."

He ended the call and turned back to the others, his gaze going unerringly to Jade before shifting to Colter. "My attorney will be here tonight or first thing in the morning with the two notes I received and, probably, the third one. I gather you've done a handwriting analysis?"

Colter's gesture sent his attention back to Jade who nodded. "Yes. Our in-house team was able to confirm that the first two notes to me and to Cargill are all a match. A scan of this last one is in their hands now. I expect we'll hear shortly."

Jonah stood and walked to the projection screen where Colter had displayed a map of the mountain peaks surrounding the ranches where Jade and Glenn had met. Jade's family ranch was notated in the valley on one side, the Hillman ranch in a valley on the other side. One peak was circled and labeled 'cabin'. A slightly higher peak to the left of it bore an X and was labeled 'body' with a question mark above the word.

Glenn shook his head almost at once. "The body fell from the peak on the opposite side of the cabin."

"Fell or was pushed?" Jonah asked as he quickly corrected the notation.

Glenn closed his eyes, watched the tumble again, some aspects still hazy, some crystalline. "The body was stiff. It didn't walk to the edge and lose balance."

Jade reached for the house phone. "Renee, do you have a few minutes to come to the Bellamy D Conference room? No rush. Thanks."

"And this was late summer, about dusk?" Colter asked.

"Early September. We were circling back to the ranchers, separating the calves born in the spring from their mothers for weaning about a month or so before turning them back out with their herds." He and Jade had been married for one week. He didn't share that bit of information. "Full dusk, most of the light came from behind the mountains as the sun sank."

Colter nodded his understanding. "Noted, but that would only make an impact of about ten to fifteen minutes on our timeline."

Jonah's mind had apparently moved in a different direction. "You were young. Did you have experience in ranching?"

"My family raised Texas beef for decades."

"So, why were you in New Mexico?"

Glenn snorted. "Pretty much the same reason we were

separating those bawling calves. My dad thought my mom was babying me, figured he'd get me out of her reach so I'd come back a man."

"Did you?"

Glenn stifled a comeback. His mind wasn't completely made up, but he had a strong feeling Jade's family wasn't, and never had been, the cause of his misfortune. All he said was, "I learned to be a man, but I didn't go home." He'd wanted to, damned if he didn't want his mama when he was battered and broken, but he hadn't let himself. Later, yeah, but not until he'd healed inside and out.

Jonah studied him a moment, and Glenn caught a fleeting glimpse of approval, approval of the boy he'd been or the man he'd become, he wasn't sure. He told himself it didn't matter, but he wasn't quite sure of that either.

They didn't get much further before a light rap drew their attention to the door. Glenn immediately stood as the woman stepped into the room.

Jade made the introductions. "Renee, thank you for joining us. This is Mr. Collier. He's assisting us with a case."

"Glenn, this is Renee Wyles. She's part of our forensics team and an expert in all things deceased … or at least all people deceased."

She was the type of woman Glenn most appreciated in a business setting. Shoulders-back confidence, a direct look and pleasant smile, a firm handshake, and a quiet but clear voice as she greeted him.

Jonah asked about her family, after which Colter asked if she had time for a few questions, inviting her to help herself at the sideboard, then gesturing for her to sit after she gave a quick shake of her head.

After the introductions, Colter took over. "Can you walk us through the stages and time sequence of rigor mortis?"

She gave him a look, and he grinned and shrugged. "So, okay, it's been a long time since my university days. I remember the generalities, but we need to get into specifics."

"No problem. Rigor mortis is a series of chemical reactions in the muscles which cause them to contract. It's typically taught as six stages. The first stage is right after death and is noted by the body's lack of stiffness, which is also true in the sixth stage. Some instructors leave off the first and final stage, teaching the process as four stages."

"What causes the muscles to uncontract?" Glenn hadn't had the benefit of university, and rigor mortis wasn't taught on oil rigs or in online finance and business courses.

"That's the beginning of decomposition," Renee answered, "when proteins start breaking down and when enzymes and bacteria begin destroying cells."

"In the first stage, when the body isn't stiff at all … how long is that?" Colter asked.

"Keeping in mind that many things affect the timing of rigor mortis, an average of two hours following death. In the third stage, many of the muscles have become stiff, even immobile, but not all of them. In the fourth and fifth stages, that process is being reversed so that by the end of the fifth stage, the last of the contracted muscles are now relaxed."

"And how long is this entire process?"

"The process of rigor mortis, starting after the initial two hours, is completed within an average of eight to twelve hours. … the process is reversed during the next twelve to twenty-four hours."

"What are the things that can quicken the process overall?"

"High ambient temperatures like summer heat.

High-energy activity in the moments before death … for example, a fatal heart attack while running."

"Or a fight … a physical struggle?" Glenn suggested.

At his question, Renee shifted her attention to Glenn. "Exactly. Anything that has the blood pumping and muscles heated from exertion. Also, a serious infection being present in the body, substance abuse, or other poisoning."

"And I suppose cold temperatures would slow the process," Jade inserted.

"Cold temperature," she agreed, "also low muscle mass in the deceased."

"So, summing it up, the body typically doesn't stiffen for the first two hours after death, and, again typically, the last of the stiffness is resolved twelve to twenty-four hours after death." Jonah said slowly.

Renee nodded. "Typically."

"Anything else you can think of that might help our understanding?"

"Not really, but if I do, I'll give a call back." Clearly recognizing she'd met the need of the moment, Renee scooted her chair back from the table.

Jade stood when she did and walked with her to the door. "Tell Robert we appreciate your time this morning."

The other woman grinned. "He says we're getting fancy new digs! We're all excited."

Jade laughed. "I guess that depends. If your idea of fancy is my idea of top-of-the-line equipment in a suite of spacious offices and labs, then be excited."

* * *

When Jade turned back to the room, she hesitated as she caught Glenn watching her. He couldn't read her expression any more than he could judge his own feelings.

Before she was settled in her seat, Simon stopped at the open door, looking uncertain. An accordion folder was clutched in his hand, and Robert was a step behind him.

"Looks like you found something of interest with that last note." Jade addressed her question to Simon since it was obvious that Robert was putting him in the lead.

The younger man took a deep breath and nodded. He glanced at the lowered projection screen and then at Colter's laptop before pulling a flash drive from his pocket. He handed it to Colter who deftly inserted it and opened the single file displayed. There were six lines of text in pairs of two, one on top of the other.

Simon squared his shoulder and nudged his wire-rimmed glasses with his forefinger. He looked at Jade as he spoke.

"The first line of text in each pair is from Set A of the notes you gave me. The second line of text in each pair is from the Set B of those notes."

"Looks like they're a match in handwriting," Colter commented. "Would you agree?"

"Almost perfectly so."

Something in Simon's tone had Jade taking a closer look. "Too perfectly?"

"In some aspects, yes." Simon gave her a glance as he spoke. "If I place them one on top of the other, almost every letter is perfectly aligned."

Glenn stood and leaned his hands on the table in front of him, studying the screen. "Almost?"

"I kept studying them because something was nagging at me." Simon pointed to several letters circled in red ink.

"I see it, now. I'm not sure I would have, but I do now." Jade looked at Simon. "The differences are random but consistent."

Simon shook his head. "Not random, scattered but infrequent enough to appear natural. Here and here," he pointed, "the S has a flaw and it's the same flaw." He pointed again. "These two places, same thing with the F."

At that, they all stood and grouped around the screen. Each of the fifth letters had a slight variation from their counterparts. Everything between appeared identical and was, from Simon's description, a perfect alignment. Jade knew no human hand could ever manage that.

"Software generated," Colter said. "So, someone computer savvy."

"Yes, sir. Without a doubt. Even more so because the program hasn't been around long and isn't much of anywhere except the underground market."

"Used for what?"

"Term papers, mostly."

"Seriously?" She lifted a brow, and he grinned.

"Professors are overworked and underpaid, right? One smart guy or gal can take a program like this and write a decent term paper. He or she then finds a different place in each copy he sells to make a deliberate error or two or substitutes a commonly used word with its synonym. Only so many copies are sold and each has at least one or two wrong answers but not the same wrong answers."

"Still, why doesn't that professor catch it?"

"Because more than a few of them hand out grading papers to a handful of favored students who mark up the wrong answers. When that professor gets them back, those red marks are in different places, so he gets a comfortable feeling that at least a semblance of care was given in the grading."

She laughed. "You think we're being blackmailed by a

college student?"

"Not impossible, but I suspect it's more likely to be someone who knows where to shop for things that could baffle law enforcement."

Glenn caught her eye. "What did that gain the blackmailer, other than us not knowing his handwriting, which he could have gotten by simply using a word document of some sort with a plain font and printing it out?"

"In terms of a successful blackmail, probably not much." Jade had asked herself the same question. "I think it says more about his ego, maybe?"

"Maybe," but he sounded dubious about that.

"Or maybe his personality," Jonah suggested. "The same as the type of person who would tediously cut the words from a magazine or newspaper and glue them on plain paper."

Glenn looked thoughtful. "Someone who has an image in his head of how a blackmailer should do things and takes the additional time to do that when a simple plain font note would do."

"Exactly. Perfectionism to the point of extreme. The same with sending three separate notes, each one building on the other."

"It builds a picture," Colter commented, "but there are still a lot of missing pieces."

"We'll find them." Not without work, Jade thought, but they would.

She shifted her attention to Simon, who had been watching all of them with rapt admiration at the back and forth. "Good work, Simon, but I guess this rules out any chance of matching anything in the state's criminal justice database."

"Thank you, Ms. Jade. It was interesting research. And, I haven't heard anything from the state yet, but, you're right, I'm not expecting any matches."

Robert got to his feet, and Simon was quick to take the hint and begin gathering his paperwork. He walked to the door, but Jade beckoned Robert aside.

He was still looking pleased. "Simon stepped it up with this one. He went beyond typical protocol and above job level in my opinion."

Jade nodded. "I would agree. Are you considering a promotion?"

He shook his head. "Not yet. Maybe in the future. I'll need to see a little more growth in that area. I think a bonus added to his check this week would be more appropriate in this instance," he said thoughtfully. "I'll get the paperwork turned in to you this morning."

"I'll approve it."

Robert's shoulders relaxed. "Thank you. He's one of the most talented I have. Not politically … he's got a lot to learn there, but he's willing, and I'll give him those opportunities."

"I trust your judgement, Robert, and I appreciate your leadership. You're building a solid team."

* * *

After lunch was brought in and placed on a side table, they filled plates and settled back to work. Glenn noticed that Jade nudged her plate to one side in favor of her notebook and pen as she studied the timeline Jonah had displayed on the screen. She made some notes, then frowned. "Still a lot of gaps."

Colter nodded agreement. "It's going to take legwork to

close those gaps. We're looking for a missing person report within a twenty-four to forty-eight-hour time frame. Plus, we're looking to find the body of that missing person. That may or may not give us motive, so we'll also be looking for motive, which may hand us the killer."

"It may also give us a lot of false leads," Jonah commented. "And all of it was information from close to two decades ago, which may have been lost, discarded, or destroyed in the years since."

Jade lifted her shoulders. "But we have to start somewhere."

Glenn agreed with their comments but kept his thoughts to himself. For now, he was in wait-and-see mode. If he agreed with the approach, he'd be all in. If not, he'd do his own digging, his own way.

Colter leaned back, dividing his attention among them as he talked. "I can make up a story about a will and a missing heir and start that missing persons search in city records. Boring, but necessary. Jonah, can you do some legwork and talk with some of the ranchers? Maybe the same kind of backstory but along the lines of a family out Arizona way looking for a son that supposedly worked here as a hand but never came home." His gaze went from Glenn to Jade and back again. "If the two of you would head up the mountain in the morning, it would help if you could pinpoint where that body fell from and was most likely to have landed. That's the point at which we need to start looking. Maybe figure out how we *do* that looking, since we can't dig up a mountainside, even if we figure out which mountain. Hell, maybe you'll get lucky and find a pile of bones that landed somewhere on its slide down."

Jonah stood and added, "And while you're up there,

could you stop in at the ranch and see how the party planning is going? Make sure things aren't getting too big and out of hand."

Jade sat silent, glaring as Colter got to his feet and asked Jonah what he could do to help with Cheney's birthday gathering.

"If looks could kill," Glenn murmured, having already decided he was in with the suggested approach.

"Oh, no worries," she retorted, still watching her cousins. "I have no intention of waiting on something so benign. There are far more entertaining ways to rid myself of them and I've considered each and every one of those ways at various times through the years." She took a deep breath. "So, how early do you want to head out in the morning?"

"Why don't we talk about that over dinner?" Glenn asked.

She turned to look at him, and he found himself holding his breath.

"That's fine," she said after a moment. "I'll meet you downstairs at 6:00."

Glenn nodded. He had plenty to occupy him for the remainder of the afternoon. He closed his laptop and stood, hesitated the barest moment, before saying, "I would never have walked away from you."

He thought he saw a glitter of tears in her eyes as he turned to go, but he didn't look back. He didn't want her to see the anguish in his.

Chapter Nineteen

Bright lights, loud music, margaritas and tacos. Glenn relaxed into the casual atmosphere as Jade was greeted by name at the front door and they were shown to her favorite booth, which proved to be one at the very back of the relatively small establishment.

Following their waiter, Jade slid onto the first bench, putting her back to the door. Glenn managed not to smile at her nod to his ego. He had a feeling she normally would have insisted on being the one keeping an eye on the door. It wasn't chauvinism on his part; it was the memory of the person he'd seen watching the apartment building.

Likely, that person had nothing to do with an old murder and blackmail notes. The Bellamys stuck their noses into all kinds of business, their own, and that of their clients. Hell, how many companies had their own forensic lab? Still, Glenn couldn't quite convince himself that the watcher was unconnected.

It wasn't until after her first margarita that Jade spoke of something other than the menu and other good places to eat in and around Albuquerque. "New Mexico has a rich history and tons of museums, if you're here long enough to venture further than the city limits," she added.

Glenn studied her expression. "I don't think we'll get to the bottom of those notes in a day or two."

She stared at the ice in her glass before lifting her gaze to his. "I know Jonah and Colter can be forceful, but you don't have to get involved, Glenn. Your future is elsewhere. You belong to someone else now. I'll sign those papers and you can get on with your life. You can leave it with us. It's what we do."

He couldn't tell if that was what she hoped would happen. If so, she was going to be disappointed. "Not happening. I don't dump my problems on other people."

"It's both our problem … and Cargill's as well. And we're not other people. We're professionals."

"And you're my wife." He said it with intentional bluntness, saw the flash of pain in her eyes. He softened his tone. "We're both neck deep and doubtless in some kind of danger without even knowing the whys or the wheres. I won't leave here until I know you're safe."

She studied his face and slowly nodded. "I guess we're going back up the mountain tomorrow then."

"First, we need to go to the valley, talk with your parents. I owe them a long overdue apology, and we both owe them an explanation."

He thought she'd argue; instead, she signaled their waiter for another margarita by lifting her empty glass. He didn't mind that the waiter brought two.

With a faint grin, he lifted his glass toward hers, and they bumped rims.

The food was as good as the drinks, but they both stopped at that second margarita, paid the check, and began the walk back.

"I think Simon has a crush on you," Glenn said.

Jade rolled her eyes at the comment. "Simon is crushing on a new lab. They all are. I'm nothing more than the means to an end."

She glanced up, catching his smile and the small shake of his head in the glow from the streetlight overhead. "Not just Simon, his boss as well."

"I'm grateful for Robert. I started in forensics … crime scene investigation … my goal was always to be on the scene, but then due to staff failures, I got caught up in the data analysis aspect and the staff management and the … well, everything." Her voice slowed as she remembered some of those days.

"And along came Robert?"

"Not exactly. I went through two team leads before he walked into my office for an interview. The first failure was a female who had never learned to combine humanity or humility with her knowledge and her skill. Her team hated her. The second failure was a male who wanted to be a best buddy to his team and did more to interfere in their daily routine with his hands-on approach than to help, sort of a benign dictator. I had to let both of them go. And I absolutely hate firing people. And then there was Robert."

"Who was just right," Glenn's tone was droll.

"We had growing pains," she admitted wryly. "But he wanted it, and he was willing to listen … to me as well as his team. They'd jump through hoops of fire for him, now."

"And you?"

"I'd make those same jumps. He keeps things smooth; each of his team knows their job, and they perform at top level because they want to make him proud. And he *is* proud of them, and he shows it at every chance he gets."

"And you get to be out and about."

"I do, and I love that I can be," she admitted.

They stopped at the corner, and Glenn pressed the crosswalk button. "I guess that's pretty much what we'll be doing tomorrow."

She studied what she could see of his expression in the shadowed light. "Are you sure you want to do this?

"Find a killer?"

But she knew he'd understood her meaning. Finding that killer might prove more physically demanding than facing her parents, but they'd both learned long ago that emotional challenges were far more devastating.

He turned to face her, and their gazes caught and held. He lifted his hand and brushed her hair from her cheek. In the next instant, he took both of them to the sidewalk, knocking the breath from her and turning so that his body covered hers as a car sped by and bullets sent adobe chips flying from the wall of the building behind them.

"Jade! God, Jade! Are you hit?"

A siren sounded as blue and red emergency lights flashed from the parking garage below their apartments, and a guard ran to the middle of the street, firing shots at the car as it raced away. Giving up, he hurried to the sidewalk.

"Ms. Jade, are you hurt? Are either of you hurt? The

police are on their way. Do we need an ambulance?"

But it was Glenn she replied to as soon as she caught her breath. "Not hit. I'm okay." Then, "No ambulance, Mr. Velasco, I promise."

Minutes later, both ends of the block were cordoned off by police cars, lights flashing but sirens silent. The chief of police glared at everyone while one detective questioned Jade and Glenn on anything they may have seen or heard during those few seconds, and two more efficiently retrieved bullets buried in the side of the building.

Jonah stood listening to the questioning with his arms crossed and his jaw set, while Colter talked on his phone and paced.

* * *

Glenn kept his arm around Jade and half of his attention on the chief, knowing any real news would come through him, so he was watching when the chief stepped back to take a call. He didn't look happy as he pulled one of the detectives from the bullet search. As the detective walked away, the chief walked back.

"We've had reports of at least two more drive-by shootings. No one injured. One, a few blocks from here, shattered a living room window, but fortunately no one was home. Then another in the north valley neighborhood right in front of Director Cargill's house. Looks like the perp was making a swing through town, maybe got on the interstate to get the hell out of Dodge."

Jonah shot a warning glance to Glenn, before he gave a small shake of his head and asked, "Was Cargill home at the time?"

"Yeah, he's plenty spooked, so I'll head over there if

y'all have what you need here. I'll leave these guys and try to round up some off-duty officers on my way. Stupid punk kids, and I doubt we'll ever get our hands on them."

* * *

An early evening turned into a late night as they regrouped upstairs. Glenn wasn't surprised to see sandwiches and coffee and even slices of cake. He also wasn't surprised to see two of the clan patriarchs, Marcus Slade and Reginald Bellamy, easily recognizable from the research he'd done. He was, however, surprised to see his attorney.

"Ellie," he said in greeting.

She lifted one brow and nodded, before her gaze shifted to Jade.

"Found her at the end of the block, trying to get past an officer," Marcus said by way of explanation.

"I owe you, then," Glenn acknowledged.

"Damn sure do, for that and more," Reginald growled. "Didn't even get an invite to the wedding."

Glenn winced, then slid a look toward Jade who divided a murderous glare between her cousins before asking, "Since it appears that everyone has been briefed on everything, anyone else want to air their complaints before we try to figure out who shot at us?"

"I expect your parents will have one or two, but they're not here so …" Marcus told her mildly as he pushed his empty sandwich plate away and pulled a slice of cake toward him. He turned his attention to Glenn. "Might as well eat. That steak sandwich was particularly good."

"Maybe coffee," Glenn said, helping himself. After the comment on the wedding, it had been an easy decision not to mention the fact that he and Jade had been returning from tacos and margaritas when that shooting occurred.

"For now," Jonah said, "we're publicly and officially going with the chief's theory that this was a handful of foolish kids."

Colter caught Glenn's frown and added, "If we even hint at anything else, Cargill's going to get wind of it."

"Why keep our suspicions from Cargill?" Glenn asked.

Marcus snorted. "Are you kidding? He's a politician. He'll let something— probably the wrong something— slip while he's making political hay about almost being gunned down. Although I agree with the lead detective. If whoever took those shots was looking to kill, he'd be dead just like you would."

Glenn considered that. "So ... a warning of some kind?"

"My suspicion is he or she has figured out who you are ... hell, might even have followed you here from the Keys ... and if you're here in New Mexico poking around with us, you aren't exactly planning to shell out extortion money and likely neither is Jade. I'd say it was as much a reminder as a warning."

Glenn shook his head. "I'll agree with you on everything except whoever the hell this is following me from the Keys. He knows too much about your family, this business, even the town, for this little stunt tonight. I haven't been here long enough for him to be that well-versed."

Marcus gave him a nod of respect. "And I'll agree with you there. So," he shifted his glance between Glenn and Jade, "what's your game plan?"

And then, he sat still and listened, Glenn gave him that. Both of them, he thought, watching the looks that crossed the faces of the two older men as first Jade, then her cousins, shared their plans. In the end, though, Reginald's gaze came back to Glenn. "You good with all of this, son?" And that question surprised him.

"I am." And it was true, he realized, he was. It wasn't his nature to trust many people. He trusted Ellie, his work crews, and Lizbeth, but few beyond that. But these Bellamys ... the people, this family, he'd despised for so many years ... he trusted as well.

"What do you need from us?" Marcus asked.

"Keep the hounds quiet," Colter said without hesitation.

"No leaks, no leads, no comments," Jonah emphasized.

"Done," Marcus said, and Reginald nodded.

"Jade?" Reginald spoke her name softly.

"I'm fine, Uncle Reggie. I love you both and appreciate your support."

Marcus cleared his throat and took a breath. "We don't know what mess you're in, Jade, but you know we have your back."

"I do know," she said before glancing at Glenn. "I need you to have Glenn's back as well. Whatever is happening is likely to be more Bellamy dirty laundry than his."

Marcus nodded. "You have that. He has that."

But Glenn thought of the stiffened body falling end-over-end and suspected his part in the deadly hunt was far greater than the fact that he'd married a Bellamy darling.

Chapter Twenty

Jade's uncles left first, then Jonah and Colter, all headed home to wives and peace and sleep. She and Ellie and Glenn were left with the ever-present reality of Glenn's fiancée, Lizbeth. Ever-present at least for Jade, like an entity hovering in the room.

Her impression of Ellie was one of determination combined with fierce loyalty. Glenn was her client, and Jade might well find herself under a steamroller if Ellie considered her a threat to Glenn. She wasn't. She'd sign the divorce papers when he got around to that, which likely wouldn't be until their blackmailer was safely jailed.

As if their thoughts had followed the same trail, Ellie pulled out a manila envelope and an unopened letter and placed both in front of Glenn who slid them both to Jade.

"No point muddying things with my fingerprints again," he said.

She glanced at the unopened letter, familiar handwriting, no return address. "I'll get these to Simon."

Then she sat quietly as Glenn explained to his attorney what they were up against and how they suspected a blackmail scheme was linked to their past.

"But no idea how this Cargill guy figures into it?"

"Not yet, nor does he know that we've also received the same notes."

Ellie pondered that a moment. "Interesting. Would you have eventually tied those notes to your past here if Jade hadn't also received them."

"No," Glenn admitted. "I'd still be trying to figure out what the hell they were about. I didn't fully accept they were blackmail notes until I found out Jade had the same first two and saw the third one here." He tapped the envelope in front of Ellie. "I'm confident this is my third one … the demand for money."

"So, from what I heard, Colter is going to dig into law enforcement records, look for someone reported missing. Jonah is going to talk with landowners in the area. The two of you are going to begin a search of the mountain in the morning. I suspect that will take several days. What can I do to help?"

Glenn lifted his hand. "You and Wesley need to take that vacation I mentioned. When is he joining you?"

Jade saw the tension as soon as Ellie lifted her chin, heard the tightness in her response. "He isn't. I don't have anything pressing in the office for the next week, and I'd rather be here than there. All I need to know is how I can help. I have a room on the north end of town."

"Have you checked in, yet?"

Ellie lifted a wary brow at Jade's question. "No."

"Good. If you'll give me your keys, I'll have security bring your bags from your car and the keys to one of the suites here."

With a glance at Glenn, who nodded, Ellie slid her keys across the table. Jade walked to the window as she placed a call downstairs, then waited near the door for the guard, giving them privacy for whatever Ellie chose to share with her boss.

When she returned, Glenn was suggesting Ellie research land ownership on each side of the mountain, starting two decades back through current.

"That's a really good thought," Jade agreed. "The timing of this is damned peculiar, considering that you're back in New Mexico when no one here could have known you would be. It might be related to a change in ownership, whether through inheritance or transfer of some kind."

Ellie nodded. "The timing *is* odd. Something changed for someone."

Jade thought she appeared at least a little pleased with the idea of a meaningful task to keep her busy.

* * *

The plan for the next morning was a brief stop by Jade's office to take the notes Ellie had brought to Simon and then get Ellie established with a computer and Jade's staff for any assistance or information she might need.

That plan fell apart when Jade stepped from the elevator and found the city attorney leaning against the receptionist desk outside her office. Even so, she greeted him with a smile as she unlocked her door with a glance at Ellie as she gestured toward the seating area near the windows. "I won't be more than a moment, if you'll make yourself comfortable."

"Come in, Leo. I'm afraid I don't have a lot of answers for you yet," she closed the door behind them before adding, "or Cargill."

"I didn't really expect answers this soon although Cargill is hoping sooner rather than later. Unfortunately, he's received another note, this one unpleasantly more pointed." He hesitated. "He's not handling this well, Jade. He's been late to the office several times lately and looks like hell when he gets there. Worse, he missed a key meeting this week. I found him afterward, sitting in his office and staring out the window."

Instead of sitting behind her desk, Jade gestured toward the small table near the window. "I'm sorry to hear that, but I won't say I'm surprised. Something like this would rattle the steadiest of people." She sighed. "And I hate to say it, Leo, but there could be more after this, with more pointed threats."

Leo grimaced. "Or something even more disagreeable than a note."

"Unfortunately, that's possible."

He pulled the envelope from his portfolio and handed it to her.

She laid it aside and met his anxious gaze. "I won't muddy the waters with my fingerprints. My staff is aware this is top priority even though they don't know why or who is involved."

Not looking any happier, Leo nodded. "We're confident in your discretion. We're also confident you have the best team that money can—or can't—buy. But ..."

"As fast as we can, Leo. I promise."

He got to his feet. "I know."

She watched him walk out and felt bad for the slump in his shoulders. Turning, she picked up Cargill's envelope and pulled the manila folder that held the notes Glenn had been sent from her briefcase. She made a quick call to the lab, then stepped out of her office. She beckoned to Ellie before heading for the elevator.

"I gather that was about a third note," Ellie said.

"It was. Expected, but ..."

Simon smiled faintly as they entered and she introduced Ellie, but he let his disappointment show soon enough. "I thought I'd have more for you by now."

Jade chuckled. "We didn't think this would be easy. Baby steps lead to big steps, but," she admitted, "I'm as frustrated by the lack of leads as you are. Keep digging. Meanwhile, I have four more notes for you." She handed him Cargill's first. "This goes with set A, and this," she touched the manila envelope she placed on his desk, "is set C. One of those three is in a separate envelope, still unopened."

Simon nodded. "So, I'll have all the prints pulled and writing comparisons made by end of day."

"I don't expect you'll find much new except the prints on set C. That person is from out of state, but I believe you'll only find one set on those." She couldn't share Simon's enthusiasm, but she appreciated it. "I'll be out of town for a day or two, and I'll need you to be Ellie's go-to until I'm back. All of her research will need to be done from one of our encrypted desktops."

She turned her glance to the other woman. "I know you'll need to access land titles in several areas." She smiled. "From there, you'll have to figure out what else, but Simon can help make sure you get what you need."

Simon stood a little taller at the idea of being Ellie's

source. Jade had no doubt she was leaving Ellie in good hands.

As she returned to her office, Glenn messaged that he was waiting for her on the street-level. Parked illegally. For some reason that addition made her smile.

Jade made a few more stops on her way downstairs, checking in with employees and co-workers, spending a few minutes getting updates or arranging support. As she shifted her briefcase from one shoulder to the other and lifted her laptop and overnight cases from the trunk of her car, the enormity of the next few days hit hard.

Once upon a time, she and Glenn had plotted how they would break the news of their marriage to her parents. She'd never dreamed that revelation would occur so many years later.

With a sigh, she walked from the shadow of the parking garage into the morning sun. Glenn stood with his hip propped against a truck she assumed was rented. Somehow, he seemed to know she was there. When he turned and smiled, her heart tripped, and she nearly stumbled. She drew a breath, glad she'd already slid her sunglasses in place.

"Ready?"

His smile held steady, and she returned it with a nod. "Ready."

But all she could think was how would she get through the next few days. All the anger she'd felt through the years had made it easier, bearable. The anger had been ripped away by the truth of what he'd suffered. All that remained was her Bellamy training to keep her cool and steady and strong.

It would be enough, she told herself, as she placed her things in the backseat and climbed up into the truck. "Was this the biggest truck they had at the rental business we use?"

This time his glance held a grin. "Not a rental. I called a dealership Jonah recommended and told them what I wanted. They had it delivered first thing this morning, full tank of gas, ready to go."

Boys and their toys, she thought, as she fastened her seatbelt. But for some reason, the thought held no derision. It held, instead, a bittersweet regret. They'd both missed out on so much in their late teen years, what they might have had if Glenn hadn't been forced away from her. Marriage was a big step, and she'd never know if they'd truly been ready for the road ahead.

But they would've had each other, and she couldn't help but believe that fact would have made everything work out for them.

* * *

Glenn had deftly merged with traffic on the interstate before he asked, "How do you think this is going to go?"

"With my parents, you mean." It wasn't really a question. The meeting ahead had to be on his mind as much as hers. He'd always liked and respected her parents and had been more fearful of their reception of him than she had ever been.

He nodded, not adding anything to the question.

She thought about that for a moment—not that she hadn't already—but thought about it from Glenn's perspective, rather than hers, about his possible reception once they arrived.

"If we were still those crazy teens, I'd be quaking in my boots from the thought of my daddy's disappointment and my mom's fiery response at me having disappointed him."

"What were his dreams for you?'

"Taking over my share of the ranch." She turned to look out the window and blinked away the tears that threatened.

But, even without seeing them, he seemed to know, and his tone softened. "And?"

"As soon as I had my equivalent high school degree, I began a four-year university program at the same time I began interning with the company. I transferred my share of the ranch equally to my brothers when I was twenty-one."

"And now it all belongs to Morgan. Any regrets?"

She felt his glance as she stared at the mountains, hazy in the distance. "Not really. I know I'm where I'm supposed to be, and I love what I do."

"Will your brother want to keep the ranch going when your folks retire?"

She smiled. "*If* they ever retire … but, yeah, Morgan and I are both content with how we get to spend our days."

"Content?"

"Sounds tepid, doesn't it?" She shook her head. "The reality is far from that. There are days that are high with success and some that are low with disappointment, but they're never boring. My contentment comes from knowing I'm good at what I do, that what I do matters, and that I'm a key asset of the Slade Agency."

None of which, Glenn thought, she would've had if she'd left New Mexico for Texas with him. He was glad to see their exit sign and shifted lanes for the ramp, leaving the interstate and their conversation behind.

Chapter Twenty-one

Melissa Bellamy-Davidson was a striking woman, and—at eighteen—Jade had been catching up to her fast. Both had timeless features, with wide cheekbones and strong yet feminine jawlines. Both had dark hair, although Missy's was threaded with silver at the temple.

Jade must have messaged as they were nearing the ranch because her mother stepped from the house to the wide verandah before Glenn had the truck in park. She watched as they exited the truck and held out her arms to Jade for a hug.

When she turned toward Glenn, her eyes, as dark as her hair, were watchful but not unfriendly. For the first time, Glenn felt more glad than irritated that Jade's cousin had told her parents, glad *that* particular conversation didn't lie ahead. None of this would be easy, but maybe not quite as difficult for Jade as it might have been.

"You're Glenn Collier."

"Yes, ma'am."

"I'm Missy." He took the hand she held out to him and was surprised when she pulled him close enough to hug, and even more surprised when she grinned and said, "Don't expect my husband to hug you."

"Mama," Jade cautioned warily.

"Don't 'mama' me. Married at eighteen and never a word. All those years before, and since, he planned to walk you down that aisle. I planned to help you choose a wedding dress." She looked from Jade to Glenn. "Calvin is on the back porch with the grill going. Go straight through the living room and the kitchen and take a couple of long-necks from the fridge when you go. Opener is on the counter to the right. Jade and I are going to sit here for a bit, whether she wants to or not."

Glenn didn't think he'd ever seen Jade with nothing to say. Until now. He did as he was told and grabbed and opened those bottles before stepping out to the porch. Jade's father sat in a straight-back chair beside what had to be an antique table and eyed the beer before reaching out a hand to take what Glenn offered.

"Have a seat."

Glenn recognized Jade's father from his days sorting calves from their mamas. He was older, and it showed in the lines on his face and the gray in his hair, but he was as lean and muscular as he'd been in his younger years. Glenn waited until the other man took a drink of the beer before he pulled out the chair opposite him.

"You're Glenn Collier."

In another time and situation, Glenn might have

chuckled at both mother and father using the same opening statement. This was not that time or that situation.

"Yes, sir."

"My son-in-law."

Glenn hesitated, then nodded. He wasn't often at a loss for words, but today was a good day for it.

"Hell of a thing to find out your daughter's married to someone you never really knew." He cut Glenn a look. "If I were younger, I woulda' kicked your ass over that."

"Someone beat you to it," Glenn offered dryly.

"And ain't that a hell of a thing? You're family, so reckon I'll have to kick their ass, instead."

Glenn took a deep breath. Apparently, Colter hadn't bothered to mention to Jade's dad that he'd arrived with divorce papers for Jade to sign. Damned if he'd bring that up now.

"Of course, I'll have to find 'em first."

Glenn decided to leave that one alone as well, and they finished their beer in silence.

The other man set his empty bottle aside and said, "I'm Calvin Davidson."

"Yes, sir, I remember you."

Calvin nodded. "I remember you just as well, and I remember my daughter making calf-eyes at you. You were a hard worker." He shifted and sighed. "I wouldn't have minded you making calf-eyes back when you were both a little older."

"Teenagers are stupid," Glenn suggested, dryly.

"I reckon they've got sense enough … when it's their brains doing the thinking." Calvin stood. "I'm going to get the steaks. Want to step back in with me and grab another couple beers?"

Glenn thought about the task he and Jade had come

to do, then thought 'what the hell'. Tomorrow was another day. He stood and followed Jade's dad back into the kitchen.

By the time Jade and her mother joined them on the porch, Calvin announced he was almost ready to pull the steaks off the grill and asked Missy if this was all they were eating.

Missy gave him a look as she said, "You know better than that."

Calvin smiled as he followed her back into the kitchen.

"And how did that go?" Jade asked quietly.

"Not bad." He met her glance, thinking, not bad at all, considering how it could have gone.

As her mother handed plates and flatware then glasses of tea to them from the kitchen door, he and Jade placed them on the table. The steak that Calvin pulled from the grill took up most of the plate in front of him, but Glenn was wise enough to put as much from the side dishes as space allowed and give equal attention to all. It wasn't a hardship; Missy was a good cook.

They talked of weather and cattle and the oil industry until Missy asked, "What are your plans?"

And, that, Glenn thought was the million-dollar question regardless of which direction this was headed. With a glance, he shifted answering it to Jade.

Jade held steady. "Regarding?"

"Colter said you were headed up the mountain … that something happened besides someone beating the hell out of Glenn up there … and you were looking for answers."

This time it was Jade who yielded to him with a look. Because she didn't answer to deflect, he understood she trusted them implicitly … they weren't just her parents, they were part of the Bellamy clan and that meant something to all of them. But this was his story, and she was letting him make the decision. Trust or not trust.

He was beginning to understand this family in a way he hadn't expected he ever would. He nodded at Jade and began to talk, disclosing everything except the blackmail notes.

When he was done, Calvin frowned. "So maybe a murder and maybe someone back then thought you saw, and maybe they think Jade did as well?"

"More maybes than anything else," he admitted. "It's a long shot."

Calvin grunted. "Doesn't seem that long a one to me, if you accept this family didn't do you any harm."

"I've accepted that," he acknowledged, "but still, even I know how much of a kid I was back then, one with plenty of imagination, and there was the lightning and the heavy clouds as the sun was going down."

"But you saw something," Missy persisted.

"I saw something,"

He hadn't mentioned the blackmail notes intentionally, primarily because he suspected Jade's cousin hadn't, but there was also Cargill, whom he hadn't yet met, to consider.

He considered it telling when Jade didn't mention them either as she added, "We're hoping that something will trigger an additional memory ... another piece to the puzzle."

"Are you also thinking you might find other evidence down the mountain?" Missy asked. "Maybe a belt buckle or cigarette lighter ... something?"

"Maybe, and also a long shot."

Calvin rubbed his chin. "Any bones would have long since been scattered by wildlife."

Or buried under a rockslide triggered by the fall. Glenn thought it but didn't say it out loud. Not in front of Jade's parents who had lost one of their sons to a rockslide.

"You're not thinking of taking that fancy truck out there mountain-climbing, are you?"

"No, sir. We should be able to park near the base each morning and spend most of the afternoon hiking up."

The older man nodded. "That should work. Some of it … maybe a lot of it … will be slow going."

"From what I recall of the terrain, I'm expecting it will be," Glenn agreed.

Missy got to her feet and picked up one of the serving bowls. "A few years back, we turned the bunkhouse closest to the foot of the mountain into a rental cottage." She turned to Jade, "The one at White Creek. I took fresh towels and linens out when I learned you were coming. There's food enough, but I'd like for you both to come back for meals here until you've done what you need to do and, hopefully, found what you need to find."

Glenn glanced across the table at Jade, who looked as uncertain as he felt. He'd expected Jade to stay here with her parents, and he'd planned to check into a small motel he'd seen listed some miles out. It seemed Calvin and Missy shared a different opinion. And it would make it easier to be close to the areas they wanted to search.

Seeing their exchange of glances, Missy shrugged. "It's got two rooms, each with their own baths and showers. After all this time, finding you're still married, you'll have things to talk through if you haven't already, things to resolve. How you resolve them is up to you." With that, she carried the bowl she was holding back into the house.

Jade was quiet, almost subdued, Glenn thought, as they all helped clear the table. This wasn't a side he'd ever seen of her, and when her father nudged him back toward the porch, he followed with a sense of relief until the older man spoke.

"You two need to head on out to the cottage as Missy calls it … make sure it has everything you need. She needs a little time to absorb what she *thought* she knew with what she knows now. Come back tonight for dinner or let us know you're not." He stopped a moment, then added, "I have a hunch there's more to your being up here than what you've said, but I'm fine with that. Keep my girl safe and let her do the same for you. She's pretty damned handy with her gun." He almost smiled. "Taught her myself for all the fancy classes she's had since."

Apparently, Jade and her mother had much the same conversation because when she stepped out later, she hugged Calvin and told him goodnight before turning to Glenn. "I told Mama we'd get settled and eat at the cottage tonight, but be back for breakfast before heading up the mountain for the day, if that's alright with you."

Glenn suspected anything would work for him as long as it didn't involve more mine-laden conversation.

* * *

As it turned out, there wasn't much conversation, at least not close-up and personal enough to be riddled with hazards. They hauled their few belongings into the cottage, which proved far more than that in size and interior design but still rustic in looks on the outside, then eased the truck through the small herd of horses, looking for Jade's favorites and debating the merits of first one, then the other for their use on the mountain should there be a need. After that, they spent what was left of the daylight hours, choosing saddles that fit each of them as well as the horses that had made the final cut.

True to her word, Missy had stocked the kitchen with easy to make food selections, but neither were in the mood to cook, nor were they really hungry. Jade found what she called her favorite gruyere beside a bottle of chilled Chardonay in the fridge and Glenn pulled a Cabernet and crackers from the pantry. They made do with that in front of the television they didn't bother to turn on.

"Should we make conversation or something?" Jade asked.

Glenn laughed but when he turned his gaze her way, the laughter faded and his throat tightened. Their story had ended a long time ago, but he knew he'd forever left a part of himself behind here in New Mexico.

"Probably not," he said quietly "It's peaceful in here, right now."

She smiled wistfully. "We could have been something."

Yeah, Glenn thought, they could have been.

Chapter Twenty-two

Glenn stepped into the cabin with a handful of wildflowers and felt that quick sense of homecoming. It wasn't their place, of course, and he didn't know where their place would be, but that was what he wanted more than he'd ever wanted anything. A place of their own, to make a life and raise a family. It wouldn't come easy. Age was against them, and Jade's parents might be against them as well.

Every time he had the thought, his mind told him how impossible it all would be, except his parents had married just as young and were still crazy in love. He was the last of five boys, and all four of his brothers would help him and Jade make a start together. His folks already had a piece of land set aside for him, and they'd promised a starter herd whenever he was ready to settle down. He was ready.

He saw two problems ahead. His piece of land was in Texas

and a long way from here. Added to that, Jade maybe wasn't ready for marriage and maybe unwilling to move that far from her home. He'd stay here and gladly but it would mean starting with little to nothing.

Looking around, he placed the wildflowers in a small bucket of water on the rickety table that centered the room, then pulled the two equally unsteady ladderback chairs out to the porch. He heard Jade riding up the trail before he saw her. His anxious thoughts eased as he stood and waited, listening to the distant sound of a songbird. They'd make it work.

In the end Jade made it all easy, sitting in his lap as they watched the sun slip lower, both knowing it was time to leave, neither wanting to make that ride down the mountain.

"This can't end," she said softly.

"Not what I want," he admitted.

"I don't mean just this moment," she insisted. "I mean us."

Glenn couldn't speak past the knot in his throat.

"I want to go with you," she whispered as she snuggled against his shoulder. "I want to go back to Texas when the work ends and you have to leave."

He wrapped his arms tighter. "Are you sure? We'd have a place to live—our own place—but it wouldn't be what you're used to. Not at first."

"As long as I'm with you, a one-room cabin will be fine. What we want, what we have in the future, we'll build together."

"Your folks won't agree to that." He was more certain of that than he was of anything in his life.

"They will if we're married."

He was as dubious as she was confident, but two weeks later they stood in front of a preacher and made their vows.

Afterward, Glenn hated every moment watching her ride down the mountainside to her family's ranch, but he did it, and he was waiting and watching later as she rode back up in the dark, unsaddling and tethering her horse before they ran, hands clasped, back into that *cabin for their wedding night.*

Chapter Twenty-three

Jade shook her head at the table laden with pancakes, bacon, and eggs, all in warming dishes, and groaned. "Mama, it's just me and Glenn … not a squad of detectives."

"You still have to eat and so do we."

"And it looks amazing," Glenn said, taking a chair.

"It does, and smells just as good," Jade agreed, giving in and stifling a 'but' at the end of the sentence. There were plenty of dogs in the yard who wouldn't mind battling over what was left. Instead, she asked how Cheney's party planning was going and what could she do to help.

"It's coming along, and your dad and I have a handle on things."

"And you're keeping it small, right?"

"Small enough."

"Mama, don't get me choked over this."

Missy sighed. "It's as small as it can possibly get for a Bellamy gathering. Colter's folks and Jonah's. Maybe a few others, but I'm not a miracle worker."

Calvin turned from the bar where he was pouring himself another cup of coffee. "You darn sure are." He leaned down to kiss his wife's forehead on his way back to his chair. "You don't listen worth a damn, but you work miracles just fine."

He glanced toward Jade. "What about getting this Declan fella back to New Mexico? Is Jonah working on that?"

"He is, and I've got my fingers crossed," Jade admitted. Declan was as close to family as Cheney had left except for the one she'd married into.

"Did you ask Jonah about the cake?"

Jade stared at her blankly. "Cake? Well … birthday cake, I guess."

"Whose child are you?" Missy asked. "Never mind. I'll call Jonah. Your dad's going to grill steak and ribs and hamburgers, and I've got the rest covered. You said no decorations, so nothing to do there."

All Jade could do at this point was pray it was as quiet a day and as small a gathering as Cheney would be comfortable with, or Jonah really would strangle her.

She was grateful when Glenn changed the subject as he helped himself to another cup of coffee. "I'm sure Jade mentioned we picked out a couple of horses in case it comes to that."

Her father leaned back in his chair. "She did. I'm hoping you'll find what you're looking for without a lot of trouble, but if you need help, Missy and I will head up to give it. Speaking of which, I'd appreciate your cell phone number and would feel better if you had mine … if you don't mind."

Glenn gave his number as he pulled his phone from his pocket to enter Calvin's. Jade didn't miss that her mother captured his number as well. She understood. She was their little girl. No matter how well-trained she was, no matter how skilled at her work, there would always be that edge of worry for them.

When it was time to go, she hugged her parents, saw that worry up close but unvoiced as they hugged her in turn. When her father shook Glenn's hand, it became more than handshake when he clapped Glenn on the shoulder and said, "Remember, you have my number."

"I'll remember." Glenn eased the moment with a grin, adding, "It's the only one on speed dial."

Jade stepped up into the passenger side as he swung up behind the wheel. He pulled out slowly as a couple of the hounds took their time moving out of the way. His gaze was on the low-country hills stretched ahead of them, cattle dotting the green. She could almost hear him thinking before he spoke.

"The Slade Agency is a part of Welles Enterprises as is the Bellamy Ranch," he said. She suspected he was talking more to himself than to her, so she didn't comment. "Your own family … this ranch …"

"Is independently owned as so many small family ranches are, but it's under contract to the Bellamy Ranch. Any ranch or farm owned by a Bellamy or a Slade or a Welles has that opportunity available to them."

"Is that opportunity limiting?"

She hesitated. "In a sense, I suppose, mostly regarding requirements for utilizing animal-friendly, health-friendly practices, which are more expensive than less careful ways, but, limited or not, it's a beneficial two-way street."

"Your brother, Morgan ... he lives close?"

"He and the youngest two of his boys are a little past those low hills, less than a mile. The oldest is in the Navy and looks to be making a career of it. It suits him."

"Are you close?"

It surprised her that she had to stop and think about that. "If he called me for help, I'd drop everything and go. I think he'd do the same for me. But ... we don't see each other often and don't have much in common. Still," she lifted one shoulder, "we're family."

"Maybe I'll have a chance to get to know him before this is all over."

She tilted her head at his comment. "You knew him back then. You worked alongside him."

"I met him. There's a big gap between meeting someone and knowing them."

She couldn't argue the point. Sometimes she felt she didn't know half the people around her.

Glenn had more than one reason for wanting to meet Morgan Bellamy-Davidson. He'd long wondered if Jade's brothers were among the men who'd held him or used him for a punching bag that night. It might have been a long time ago, but there were a couple of voices he didn't think he'd forget.

Chapter Twenty-four

Glenn had opted for starting at the bottom and working their way up. Jade had been dubious, thinking if they started at the top the going would be easier.

"Ever been rock climbing?"

Jade shook her head.

"If you're climbing up, you're looking up. You can see where you're placing your hands, choose the best spot visually, before you test it with your weight physically. If you're going down, you're testing your next foothold without seeing it or what's below it."

Giving him a dubious look, she asked, "So you do this kind of thing for fun?"

Glenn snorted. "Hell, no. I did it once during a physical skills training and that was plenty. Fortunately, most of our terrain the next few days will be forest trails and open meadows. But where there's rock, it's always safer and faster going up."

"So," she said giving his shoulder a small nudge, "let's go."

He chuckled and turned, gesturing toward the faint trail that eased up the first slope. "After you."

It was, Jade thought, a beautiful day for late spring. A flurry of storms had eased out of the area over a week ago, and the summer heat had yet to take hold. Faint breezes stirred the aspen leaves and she wondered why she didn't do this more often. By the time they took a break a couple of hours later, she'd remembered why. This wasn't her idea of fun.

She knelt at the base of an oak and slipped her backpack to the ground before shifting to lean her back against the solid trunk and looked up to find Glenn watching her with an expression she couldn't read.

He pulled a couple bottles of water from his backpack and tossed one to her.

Determined to ease the unexpected tension she felt between them, she managed a grin. "Are we there yet?"

He smiled back but before he could answer, she was pulling her vibrating phone from her pocket. Glancing at the screen, she answered, "Good morning, Robert."

He skipped the pleasantries. "I heard from Colter what you're up to. You're doing it wrong."

"Hang on." She pushed a button before continuing. "Glenn's right here. I put you on speakerphone. Say that again and explain why."

"You're doing things the hard way. I'm sending a helicopter to you with an aerial photographer. The photographer will send the photographs to you and to me. He has a couple of programs which can create maps from vertical as well as oblique aerial photographs. All you'll need to do is let me know which photographs capture a place you want to see up close. We'll map the best route to get from one place to another."

"Robert, you're a genius."

"Which is why you should have clued me in before now on what is going on. Not that I need to know the why. I don't even want to. The what was all I needed. You should hear that helicopter soon. Send me your coordinates and I'll let you know when the pilot spots the safest place for him to land closest to you and what direction you need to take to get to him. You'll need to give him an idea of what land formations you're looking for, and he'll take multiple angles for you to study." He paused. "You can trust these guys, Jade. They served together in a combat unit overseas and guarantee absolute discretion."

"Thank you, Robert. I'll be in touch, I promise." Jade broke the connection, checked her phone for their location, and forwarded the information to Robert. She took a deep breath as she looked across at Glenn. "Well … damn. Nothing like being justifiably chastised by one of your team."

He chuckled. "I'd have to agree."

For a moment she stretched flat out on the ground and stared at the sky, feeling unexpectedly content to be exactly where she was. That didn't happen often, she thought, not nearly often enough. She was always focused on the next case, the next threat, the next *something.*

She was almost disappointed when her phone alerted her to another text message. "Robert says we should head due north from our current location. The pilot will be landing in a decent-sized clearing, and they'll wait for us there."

Glenn stood first and held out his hand to her. Jade felt

odd taking it, letting him pull her to her feet.

The incline proved steep at first, and she noticed Glenn held steady a few steps behind her. When it leveled out and he moved up beside her, she realized his position had been a protective one. Before she could decide whether to be irritated or touched that he thought she might need help, she was distracted by the sound of the rotors ahead of them. The hike had been shorter than she'd anticipated.

Moments later they stepped into the clearing. The aircraft rested on level ground, rotors gradually slowing to a stop. The pilot stayed in place, but the passenger climbed down, introducing himself as he greeted Jade first, shaking the hand she extended.

"Eric Reedy, ma'am."

In turn, she introduced Glenn by name, adding, "This is really Mr. Collier's search. The Slade Agency is facilitating."

At first glance, Eric appeared little more than a kid to Glenn. A closer look at the silver edging the red hair at his temples and the laugh lines bracketing his bright blue eyes, assured him this was no greenhorn.

Eric shook his hand. "I hear we're looking for a leaf in a forest."

"More like a pebble buried in a landslide … but, yeah. Unfortunately, I don't have any exacts to give you and can't say I'll be entirely sure if and when we find what we're looking for."

Appearing undaunted, Eric nodded. "Let's give it a try and see where this leads."

Glenn took a breath. "I have reason to believe someone was killed and buried on this side of the mountain some years back. I don't expect to find anything that looks like a grave but maybe a pile of rocks out of place from where they might have fallen or even a natural fall of rocks that is oddly larger than what surrounds it." Shaking his head, Glenn added, "Sounds crazy hearing myself say it."

"Not crazy compared to some things I've helped locate. I could see a scenario where maybe two partners find something worth digging for out here, and one gets greedy. Easy to pick up a rock and…" he glanced at Jade and seemed to shift gears, "well … let fly with it. Come back later to make sure that accident is never questioned. Just this side of the mountain?"

"Yeah, but from the peak, so it could be any distance down and anywhere across the breadth."

"So, you think he was pushed to his death." The pilot scratched his head. "Well, he or she."

"I think either scenario is possible," Glenn said carefully.

"This might be our more interesting case this year. I have to be honest. I think this hunt is going to take all of this afternoon and tomorrow morning, maybe a little longer adding in refueling at the nearest airport every three or four hours. I know there's something of a rush."

"To a degree, but accuracy is more critical than speed," Jade said. "Take what time you need and let us know when you're ready for us to look at what you have."

Her phone buzzed, and she gave Glenn a glance as she stepped a few feet away before she answered.

Eric rubbed his jaw as he studied the terrain around them. "I know there are guided nature walks and hiking and horseback trails in the mountains now, but this place doesn't seem to be along a well-beaten path. Why wouldn't the killer leave the body to be found? Why come back and bury it?"

"At the time I believe this occurred, this area of the mountain was part of a working cattle ranch, several as a matter of fact. Those old-timers have mostly been bought out with a few small, scattered farms here and there."

"Sounds to me like a pretty cool murder mystery. You're not producing one of those 'true crime' type podcasts, are you?"

Glenn shook his head. "No podcast. This is personal. I'm trying to find out what happened to a guy I used to know." In a way, that was as true as any real explanation he could have given. The fact that he was the guy and what happened was the beating wasn't the mystery. The real story, the real mystery was what had he seen that night that had led to three people being blackmailed … along with the who and the why.

"Well, I hope you don't leave us hanging when our part's done. I'd like to hear when you find your answers."

"Fair enough … if we find them." And Glenn hoped like hell they *would* find them.

He watched as Jade tucked her phone back in her pocket. She glanced from him to Eric. "Slight change of plans, guys. Eric, could you bring the photographs to the Bellamy Building tomorrow afternoon for us to review … maybe one o'clock if that's convenient? We have an unexpected meeting, so Glenn and I need to go back this afternoon."

"That won't be a problem at all, Ms. Bellamy."

"Thank you. I'd like for our internal team to review these as well … see if anything jogs a memory, decide if we need any additional … before you work your magic and create a map."

Eric nodded. "I'll see you then."

They stepped back as he climbed up into the helicopter. Giving a quick wave, they walked toward the far side of the clearing, hearing the slow start of the rotors behind them.

"What's the meeting about?"

"Jonah's search for missing persons has yielded some interesting results."

"So, we have a potential?"

"We have five potentials, two of which are strong enough to make the shift to *likely*."

"Huh." Could be an interesting lead, he thought, or could prove a muddying of the waters. Either way, he'd stick this out until he could go home with answers.

Jade was quiet as they made their way back down to the truck. Once they pulled onto the road, he tried to keep his focus on traffic, but couldn't help an occasional glance her way.

As they neared the intersection that would take them to the cabin, she said, "I'll message my dad and let him know we'll be back in a day or two."

"You don't need anything from your bag?"

"Not really. You?"

He laughed softly. "Not really." He'd already discovered that if there was anything he'd failed to bring, a call downstairs had it delivered to his room within minutes. That should work equally well for anything he might have left at the ranch.

The lights of Albuquerque had started to shimmer against the night sky when they left the interstate.

"Hungry?" he asked.

Jade gave him a lazy kind of smile. "Always, but hungry is warring with sleepy."

"So, head back to our apartments? I can make do with having something delivered."

She shook her head. "No. Hunger just won the war. I suspect it always will. Are you up for sushi?"

"In New Mexico? Is this a hoax of some kind?" Although he'd been forced to acknowledge the Italian hadn't been.

"Not at all. Take the next exit, and I'll prove it."

"Sounds like a challenge to me," he said, expertly crossing two lanes of traffic on their right to get to the exit in time.

"Nice driving," she murmured.

"I learned on a dirt track."

"And that's the first thing about you that hasn't surprised me in the least," she admitted.

Kokoro's was as unexpected as about everything else he'd experienced in New Mexico. It sat on several acres of carefully cultivated land on the outskirts of the city and could have been a southern antebellum home by its architecture. The interior was typical Japanese in the minimalistic décor but without the use of paper screens or sliding doors. The only splash of color existed in a room-length mural of mostly soft silver with broad streaks of unexpected glittering gold.

Jade was greeted by name, and they were escorted to a corner, away from the groups of diners closer to the center.

Their escort asked if the location was acceptable and would they be pleased to order cocktails. Jade asked for a Blackcurrant Cassis, but Glenn asked for a beer, knowing he would limit himself to only one and not just because he was driving. He was finding it difficult to be objective about his future, difficult to keep his glance and his thoughts from drifting to Jade and their past.

Her thoughts, however, seemed centered firmly on the present, when she said, "We could be searching that mountain for more than a few days. How will your company fare without you?"

"I have a good staff, from management to craft. Which reminds me, what time is our meeting tomorrow?"

"Not until 9:00, but I can have it moved in either direction."

He shook his head. "9:00 works. I have a conference call with my lead team at 8:00. That, too, could be moved in either direction but," he shrugged, "we need to keep it brief so ..."

"All of your oil rigs are deepwater, are they not?"

"Now, they are. The first ones I worked and the first I owned were in the Texas flatlands, but I kept moving south until I reached the gulf. It appealed to me in the same way these mountains do. The scenery is different, but the appeal is the same."

He leaned back as they were served their drinks before asking, "Have you traveled much?"

She shrugged. "Here and there. A trip to France with my parents one summer. To Greece with friends during college. Otherwise, mostly quick business trips around the globe."

He watched as she lifted her drink to her lips, barely tasting it before setting it down again. When she lifted her gaze to his, her eyes glittered. "I'm so damned angry, Glenn."

He took a deep breath. He'd been wondering if they would get to this point, to blunt candidness, instead of skirting the issues of their past, of what had been done to them. "I know."

"I want to hurt someone."

That was mild compared to his own urge to rip someone's head from their neck. "Even if we find a body ... even if we learn their identity, we may never know who or why was behind that death."

She shook her head. "I won't stop until I know."

"Sometimes life doesn't give you any choice but to

move on."

She dropped her gaze from his. "Sometimes life is a witch."

And, fortunately a server arrived with their food.

Each stayed lost in their own thoughts on the remainder of the drive back. Glenn was grateful. He didn't want to know hers, didn't what to share his.

Chapter Twenty-five

Before she slept, Jade did what she'd never allowed herself to do. She looked up every article she could find on Glenn Collier, starting with the earliest, which was about seven years after he'd disappeared from her life.

An unknown in the industry, he'd sunk every dime he had into an oil well that appeared to have run dry. Risking a newly discovered and not-quite-proven technology in drilling, he'd made himself and the patent holder for that technology rich, not quite overnight, but almost.

He'd taken that money, and, without fanfare, bought several other non-producing wells with continued success. For a few years, news about him seemed sparse, then he'd re-emerged in the offshore oil industry, closing his land wells one-by-one as his offshore rigs began out-producing them.

Since that time, he'd been photographed with a host of accomplished women ... Olympic equestrians, famed surgeons, renowned artists, and jazz singers from Seattle to the Hampshires to the Keys, which he currently called home. In recent months, those women had dwindled to one, a lovely, high-fashion model. His fiancée, she assumed, although no engagement had been announced as yet.

Staring at the other woman's perfect features, Jade knew she might love again as Glenn had learned to do. She hoped she would. But it would never be what she had felt that long ago time. And maybe that was simply life. Regardless, she would survive and eventually thrive. She was a Bellamy.

* * *

Because Ellie was in town and because he had questions, Glenn asked her to sit in on his staff conference call. Being on retainer, she wasn't technically a staff member, but close enough, and he wouldn't mind changing that status if she were willing and if things with Wesley were as he suspected. He knew Collier Oil already took up more than half of her work hours.

Right before eight, he opened the door to her tap and raised his brows. Her smooth, dark hair was now a tangle of curls that included a streak of pale blue. She stepped past him with a forced smile yand placed her briefcase on the bar that separated the kitchen from the living area.

"I like the look," he said and meant it. It suited the adventurous soul he'd long suspected she kept sharply curtailed.

"I do too."

She pulled a notebook from her briefcase while Glenn

dialed into the conference call with a desk phone that provided conference capability. She eyed him curiously. "You feel that safe here?"

"Don't you?"

After a moment, she said, "I do, as a matter of fact."

The weekly call wasn't lengthy. They never were, but Glenn felt them crucial to a smooth-running team. Each rig manager sent regular reports that, although detailed, made it easy to assess the status of maintenance and operations. The calls were more about teamwork and communication. With few exceptions, this being one of those rare exceptions, he made a practice of being on one of the rigs for the call which helped keep his pilot's hours current and him in close contact with his teams.

After the call, Glenn leaned back and focused his attention on Ellie. "Want to talk?"

"Not particularly." She sighed. "But I'd like to offer you some advice."

He tilted his head. "Go ahead."

"Never go into a partnership with a lying, cheating bastard."

For a moment, he just looked at her, hating the sparkle of tears she was determined not to let fall. "Then I'll offer you some as well." He didn't wait for her consent. "Never negotiate your own divorce from a lying, cheating bastard."

Then he picked up his phone and made a call.

Ellie seemed to have herself together by the time they reached the meeting room where Jonah sat alone, scowling at a sheaf of paper in front of him. He glanced up, and his expression cleared as they walked in. "There's fresh coffee and breakfast on the sideboard, if you haven't eaten."

Glenn headed for the coffee while Ellie chose a chair. When he turned back toward the room, Jonah was putting the papers aside and Colter and Jade were walking in. Robert and Simon were close behind them.

Glenn felt an odd sense of pride when Jade took the lead at the center of the room and said, "Ellie, I'm going to ask you to step up and walk us through what you and Simon were able to discover."

Jade took a seat and, with a quick glance at Glenn, Ellie handed Jonah a flash drive. She picked up the remote control then walked to the front of the room and beckoned Simon to join her.

She started talking while Jonah inserted the drive into his laptop and pulled up the data to display on the screen behind her. "Initially, and until relatively recently, four families owned the majority of the acreage below the peak in question." With the remote, she paged through the first four screens. The family names were at the top with a family diagram beneath each one. "Some of that land remains with each of these original four, some has been broken up and sold, some has been taken over by the state under eminent domain. As I tracked those transactions, I recorded owners as well as extended family at the period of time in question, then handed their names over to Simon, who created family trees that tracked the births and deaths of each—and, in five instances—the unexplained disappearances."

"Simon." She passed him the remote.

Simon brought up the first family tree. "These are the Clintons. And this," he pointed to the name circled in bold red, "is Reagan Clinton, oldest daughter and collegiate triathlon division winner. After graduation, she set off with a backpack and a map, never to be heard from again. There's no record of death or marriage or childbirth."

"Did the parents make any attempt to locate her?"

"First through the police, then a private investigator, but neither search produced results."

Glenn shook his head with a faint frown. "Maybe, but I'm almost positive it was a man I saw falling."

With a click of the remote, Simon pulled up the next screen. "This is Reagan at her last college competition."

Glenn nodded, understanding. The photo was of a very attractive, tall young woman with a muscular build. Her hair appeared long but tightly coiled around her head. In the dark, with no features visible, she might well have appeared to be a man.

"She's one I consider likely. Another is Benjamin Wrigley," Simon said, bringing up the next family tree and a photo after that. "He left a dear Jane letter for his pregnant wife, saying that he'd met someone who 'fit him better' and he didn't think he was cut out to be a father."

"Why is he likely? That's a common enough theme these days."

"Turns out the wife had a boyfriend of her own and the baby was his, not the husband's. She got an annulment and the two of them set up a cozy little home on her ex's family property."

"Nice and neat—too neat," Jonah concurred. "Who else?"

"Lucien Montoya." Simon didn't linger over the family tree and moved on to the photograph.

Glenn studied the likeness carefully. Right build, right height, and that was all he had to go on.

"History?" Colter asked.

"A loner. He was orphaned as a young teen and raised by his grandparents, who were old-school with a real chip on their shoulder because so much of their land was lost due to property taxes the generation before them had never paid."

"So, he had that same chip?" Glenn asked.

Simon shook his head. "Not that it was recorded, but his grandfather regularly fired off letters to the local paper, the local city fathers, and state politicians. Some of them borderline threatening. He stayed on the right side of that line, but barely."

"And the two who didn't make the likely cut?" Jade asked. She couldn't see a tie between Cargill and the letters to state politicians a generation ago, but she tucked the knowledge away rather than discarding it out of hand.

For the first time Simon looked uncomfortable as he changed screens. There were two family trees side by side on this one. He clicked the remote again, and the next displayed a boy and a girl who could have been any age from fifteen to twenty. Without being told, Glenn already knew their story, knew why Simon had been reluctant. He supposed it had been inevitable there were at least whispers of his story and Jade's.

"High school sweethearts. Anna Merriweather and Ricky Westfall. He bought her an engagement ring, and her folks said 'not no, but hell no'. They left for senior prom, and no one has seen or heard from them since."

Simon passed the remote back to Ellie, who turned toward Jade. "I agree with Simon's assessment of the most likely candidates."

"I do, too," Jade said with a nod. "Well done, both of you. Robert, thank you for the loan of Simon's assistance and for calling in the helicopter service. I suspect their map will save us a tremendous amount of time. You're both welcome to stay while we review his photographs."

Smiling, but shaking his head, Robert stood, and Simon joined him at the door. "We've got another meeting shortly.

One of the APD detectives has asked us to give input on one of their cases. It should prove to be very interesting."

"Good to hear," Colter said with a nod. "Keep that goodwill and cooperation flowing."

As Ellie moved to leave with them, Jade signaled her to stay, asking, "What are your next steps?"

"At the moment, I'm combing through school, court, and hospital records for anything that stands out with those surnames. But, honestly," she shrugged, "I'm going to be surprised if we find anything significant."

"I agree; it's unlikely. Our best bet is to find the body then figure out the who and the why. If you have time to stick around, our photographer should be here about now. We're going to look at the photographs he took to determine the most likely search areas."

"I've got all the time my boss says you can have." Ellie smiled at Glenn. "This is like a giant jigsaw puzzle and the most fun I've had in a while."

He smiled back as he gave her a thumbs up, thinking Wesley damned sure hadn't deserved her. Given the chance, Glenn planned to tell him exactly that.

* * *

Eric Reedy arrived on time as Jade had anticipated he would. Instead of faded denim, his jeans were dark and as creased as only a laundry service could manage, and instead of yesterday's graphic tee shirt, he wore a polo shirt with a helicopter applique on the left side and Reedy's Helicopter & Topography Service on the right. She met him at the meeting room door and thanked the receptionist who had escorted him up. He'd emailed the photographs to her earlier that morning, and she pulled them up after introductions and an offer of coffee, water, or soft drinks, which he declined.

"If you'll walk us through, explaining where you started, we'll try to keep our bearings." Handing him the remote, she returned to her chair.

Eric proved as comfortable talking in a boardroom as he was on the side of a mountain.

"I have far more photos than I think you need, but I want you to see all of them and weigh in to be sure. The ones I've selected as appearing to be most relevant have an X in the upper right-hand corner. And by relevant, I mean the rock formations don't seem as natural to the location. That doesn't mean they aren't, which is why you need to agree or disagree."

Once they'd viewed and commented and, in some cases, discussed at length the places he'd photographed, Jade had to agree with his assessment, as did Colter and Jonah. They added a few more places to include on a 'just in case' reasoning.

Glenn appeared to scrutinize each one but had little to say. His silence reminded her that he'd been born and raised on the Texas prairies and lived most of his adult life in those flatlands or the Florida Keys. His mountain experience had been brief, devastating to both of them when all was said and done, but brief for all of that.

When they reached the final photograph, Jade stepped forward. "Thank you, Eric, these are perfect. I suspect we'll find what we're looking for in one of the places you initially indicated, but it won't hurt us to look at those we've added." She turned toward Jonah and Colter. "Thoughts?"

Colter shrugged. "More curiosity than anything." He turned his gaze toward Eric. "I don't know much about creating maps. Is this a new technology, using aerial photographs to create small, individualistic maps?"

"Not new but definitely improved. The first methods were developed in or around the 1920s. From what I've read, it was cumbersome and imperfect, just as computers were bulky and imperfect. Certainly, those early years didn't include laptops with software that could be used by non-programmers like me. The added ability to use oblique as well as vertical photographs was a big jump forward in the technology."

"Is this mapping part of your core contract services?

"As of recently," Eric said. "Previously, we were nothing more than a helicopter service. Photography was my hobby. Most of our topography customers are land developers or local governments, and the maps involve parks and recreational sites. This job was a first of its type for me." He paused. "But all of my work is strictly confidential."

Colter leaned back, looking satisfied.

Jade had one last question for Eric. "How long will it take you to create a map, one that will take us to each of those locations in the shortest amount of time?"

"The program is surprisingly fast. Because you're looking at only a small fraction of the state, you'll have it within a few hours of me getting back to my computer."

"So, by morning?"

"Or sooner."

Jonah looked from Jade to Glenn. "And this will give the two of you what you need?"

At their nods, both he and Colter got to their feet and shook Eric's hand.

"We appreciate your time, and it was good to meet you," Colter said. "Let me know if you get tired of freelancing."

Eric lifted a brow in surprise. "So far this business

is what I hoped it could be, but nice to think I'd have a fallback plan."

"I doubt you'll need it, but I'm sure we'll need you again," Colter said. "I'll be in touch."

Chapter Twenty-six

Jade's phone rang as the room cleared; she asked Ellie and Glenn to give her a few minutes. Glenn waited until she'd stepped out into the hall, before turning to Ellie.

"Any news on the home front?"

"There is no home front. Not anymore."

Glenn could see pain warring with anger in her eyes. "I'm sorry. I hate this for you."

"Bastards are born, and shit happens." She shrugged. "What next?"

"On the advice of my excellent divorce attorney—and thank you for that—I paid double for a moving service to pack everything at the office and in the apartment except his clothes over the weekend while he was out of town 'on business'. The contents, furniture, everything is in a storage unit." She smiled tightly. "Well, several storage units. I terminated the lease on the apartment, effective the end of the month, and messaged a photo of him and his sweetheart with the advice to pack his stuff before the apartment manager sells it online." She smiled faintly, then shrugged. "That felt good. For a moment, anyway."

"Where did you get the photograph?"

"From a golf buddy who had a problem being asked to cover for him."

"What hurts worse?" Glenn asked cautiously. "Your heart or your pride?"

She sighed. "Damn. I've avoided asking myself that."

"You pretty much just answered. Now it's just a matter of paperwork and making a new life."

Ellie tilted her head. "What about your paperwork?"

Glenn shrugged, glad she hadn't asked about his heart versus his pride. "It's on hold for now."

She frowned, and he answered that frown. "I need answers to a lot of things, why what happened to me— and Jade, as well—happened. As much as the why, I want to know who was behind it. The other can wait."

"I'm sure by now she's done her homework and understands just how much Collier Oil is worth."

"I'm not worried about that."

"As a friend, I'm not saying you should worry, but as an attorney, I *am* saying you need to get things settled. New Mexico *is* a community property state, and Collier Oil is worth a lot."

Before he could answer, Jade walked back into the room. He knew immediately from her expression that she'd heard at least the last part of the conversation from the hall.

"Let's get back to work, shall we?" Her voice was calm,

but her expression held hurt.

Glenn wanted to answer that hurt, but he let it go. Now was not the time or place and likely there never would be. Life was a bitch. He'd learned that lesson at eighteen. And it was a lesson he never forgot.

Jade didn't sit, she simply dove into the task at hand, just as she always had from the first day he'd laid eyes on her, as he suspected she always would.

"I've got things to wrap up this afternoon, as I'd like to get an early start on the mountain tomorrow. If the two of you have time to look back through the list of our five potentials, particularly the three deemed likely, and see where their family properties are in relation to the photographs Eric thought most relevant, we may be able to shorten our search. If not, I'll tag Simon and Robert to lend a hand."

"We've got time," Glenn said, keeping his voice as even and unemotional as hers.

"Great. Thanks. I'll message you as soon as Eric sends the map. If it isn't too late, perhaps we can head back to the ranch ... the cottage ... tonight. If not, have a good evening and we'll set out in the morning."

With that, she turned and walked out with her shoulders back and her head held high.

"I'm sorry," Ellie said, looking miserable. "She heard me. I'm so sorry."

Glenn shook his head. "It's fine. I don't imagine divorce, or anything that comes with it, is ever fun and games, but our marriage, what we had, was a long time ago. We were just kids. We're older and wiser now. We'll deal with the legal trappings when the time comes, and we'll get through. Jade's tough." She had to be. And so had he.

* * *

Jade made a quick call downstairs and headed for the elevator. She nodded at an employee she passed in the hall, asked the doorman downstairs about his pregnant wife's morning sickness, and smiled at the security guard when he wished her a good morning. She let the smile fade but kept her shoulders back and her chin lifted as she climbed into the waiting taxi.

The distance to the offices of the city council was short, but every minute of the day was already accounted for and she was borrowing from Peter to pay Paul to fit in this meeting with Cargill. Even so, she felt it was necessary. He had as much of a vested interest in the outcome as any of them. Maybe more so. Not that she had any intention of providing him with more than the barest information at this point. She agreed with Marcus. She'd never known a politician capable of keeping his mouth shut if there were votes to be gained by spilling secrets. Still, he needed to hear something from her, and he deserved some kind of reassurance that she was actively looking for answers.

When the driver slid smoothly into a parking place near the front entrance, she asked for him to keep the meter running until she returned and gave him enough of a tip to ensure that he did.

A gust of dry wind swept up the dust along the sidewalk, and she closed her eyes against the grit then walked inside. No one paid much attention as she strode the length of the hall to Cargill's corner office, which was at the back of the building and away from the street noise. He looked startled to see her and not particularly pleased. He shot an uneasy glance at the busy hallway behind her.

She eased that faint look of displeasure by saying clearly, "Thank you for seeing me on such short notice, Paul. I need some advice, and then I'll get out of your hair. May I close the door?" Which she did without waiting for his answer.

Looking a little less displeased, he waved her toward a small table and joined her there.

She jumped right in by saying, "I apologize for not giving you warning, but I've been out of town on your case and I'm leaving again soon."

"Out of town?" The frown returned as he pushed his glasses up on his nose with a forefinger. "You think this isn't someone local?"

"Just following a lead … actually more hunch than lead." She leaned back in her chair and sighed. "I have to admit, I don't have a lot to go on and not a lot of new information. What I do have, however, is very unexpected."

"Let's hear it."

"You were not the only person to receive those notes."

He tilted his head. "You're saying someone else received similar notes?"

"Not similar. Identical."

Taking a quick breath, he rocked back in his chair, looking confused, then shaking his head. "That makes no sense."

"Not yet," she agreed. "Not to us, but there has to be a connection of sorts."

"This…" he stopped, rubbing his hands together anxiously. "Well, it's unexpected. I'd thought this was a political stunt of sorts. Someone who's hoping to intimidate me, perhaps get me to step down from my position."

"And it may still be."

"So, this other recipient is in a government role?"

"Non-political but very wealthy and certainly influential."

Cargill looked pained. "I'm not wealthy and my influence isn't great, but there is always someone out there who thinks he or she can do a better job than the incumbent in any office."

She smiled, trying to look reassuring. "No doubt, but the council members, indeed, the entire city, feel you are doing a great job." Having done what she came to do, she stood. "Political or private warfare, I'll find the answers you need. Meanwhile, don't answer any unknown calls … let everything go to voicemail. And, Paul, if you think you're being followed at any point or believe someone is watching your house, call in officers. Or, at the very least, call me. I'll have Jonah or Colter set up twenty-four-hour protection."

Cargill stood as well. "Thank you, Jade. I hadn't considered the possibility of physical risk."

"I don't think you need to be overly concerned. Just be cautious." She walked toward the door but turned back before she opened it to step out. "I'll be in touch. I'm sorry I don't have more to go on, but if you think of anything from your past that might have led to this, please let me know."

"Yes. Of course."

He didn't look any less stressed than he had when she walked in, but she'd done what she could for now.

She was grateful to see her cab driver leaning against the front fender. He straightened and opened the door at her approach. As much as she preferred driving herself, a quick ride downtown in a taxi was sometimes preferable. This was one of those times.

Once in her apartment, she showered off the grit that came with an Albuquerque dry spell. She towel-dried her hair and slipped into jeans and a tee, not bothering with makeup. She had no intention of leaving her apartment before morning.

Signing into her laptop, she opened her email and found the map from Eric waiting at the top. Perfect timing, she thought, noting the delivery time of twelve minutes earlier. Even before opening the file, she forwarded the email with its attachment to Glenn, with a quick, "Let me know what time you want to head out in the morning."

Chapter Twenty-seven

Irritated with himself, Glenn glanced from the darkening skyline to his watch. This made the third time in twenty minutes that he'd wandered from his computer screen and a financial review of the firm's least productive rig. The drilling consultant remained optimistic. The production supervisor grew increasingly frustrated. And Glenn, who had the most to lose, at least in terms of money, wasn't sure he gave a damn either way.

The sound of incoming mail from his laptop drew him back to the desk tucked into a corner of the living area. He checked the screen, saw Jade's name in the sender field, but didn't sit to open it. He turned toward the bar, then turned back. A shot of whiskey or glass of wine wasn't what he wanted. He'd heard people say they were homesick, not for a place, but for a time that no longer existed. He'd never been able to understand—until now.

Reminding himself he needed to focus on what was in front of him, he read the attachment Jade had forwarded from the helicopter pilot. He needed to do a lot of things. Like call Lizbeth and ask about the wedding arrangements and tell her he loved her. Like explain to Jade that Ellie hadn't meant to be insulting earlier. And put the divorce papers in front of her to sign.

Colter had said her apartment was right above his. It was more probable she was up there now, settling into an evening of work, as he'd planned to do. He glanced around the room before taking a bottle of wine and two glasses from the counter and heading for the door. He left the divorce papers in his briefcase. That, he told himself, was for another day.

Ignoring the elevator, he took the stairs to the next level and hesitated no more than a moment before lifting the rapper to knock on her door.

* * *

Jade looked at the camera image above the door. For a moment, she stood in indecision, knowing that opening that door would change things. Maybe not for him, but for her. She'd numbed herself through the years. No, she thought, not numbed … strengthened. Maybe even hardened, she admitted, never once allowing any man past the barriers she'd put in place. Oh, she'd dated, danced, flirted, enjoyed a healthy round of sex on occasion, but she'd never lowered those emotional brick walls that protected her.

The anger that had helped stack those bricks was gone.

What had been done to her ... to them ... hadn't been done by him. Maybe they could both move on from this, him to marry his fiancée, her to look at the men around her with different eyes.

With a sigh, she slipped the chain and opened the door. He stood, shoulder propped against the doorframe, as his gaze slid from her shower-tousled hair to the bare feet below her faded, straight-leg jeans. His smile held as much wariness as her aching heart.

She glanced at the wine bottle in his hand. "I could use some of that." She stepped back and he stepped in.

She gestured toward the bar in one corner, watching as he opened the foil and pulled the cork. "Did you think I wouldn't have wine glasses?"

The glance he gave her held a rueful humor. "I'm not sure I did much thinking at all."

She didn't know what to make of the comment, so she stayed silent as she sank back onto the deep cushions of her sofa, tucking her bare feet under her. He handed her one glass and sat beside her, not distant, but not too close, either.

Leaving the ball in his corner, she took a sip of her wine and murmured, "Nice."

"Whoever stocked the apartment has good taste," he acknowledged, before picking up that ball. "I'm sorry for earlier ... Ellie is a lawyer. She thinks like a lawyer. Sometimes she comes across as a hard-ass lawyer. She's not. She admires you, and she feels bad that she insulted you."

"I get it," she admitted. "It stung in the moment, but I do get it, and I got over it." She lifted her glass. "A peace offering wasn't necessary but I appreciate the thought."

The silence that fell was more peaceful than she would

have expected. Once upon a time, she'd pictured days like this. Images of her parents, sitting together on a worn leather couch—not because they couldn't afford better but because it was the known and the familiar—had been her inspiration. She stifled a sigh for all the stolen dreams.

"Did you get the email I forwarded from Eric?"

"The map? I did. I didn't open it, but it came through."

"We could look at it now, if you want … maybe decide where to start in the morning and what time we want to head out."

"Sure."

Glenn got to his feet when she did and followed her to an office that was almost as large as her living area and seemed to be a lot more lived in. "I think we should start by notating the names of all five potentials on their family properties, but focus our search on the three likeliest."

"Good suggestion."

He pulled out his phone. "Hold on a sec, I've got notes on what Ellie and I sketched." He pointed at the screen in front of her. "This first area, the Clinton girl."

"Reagan," she murmured.

"Then about a fourth of the way east is Wrigley," he said, pointing again. "From the middle to the far side would be the family of those sweethearts whose property adjoined."

She looked up, frowned. "What about Montoya?"

"His land was actually on the other side of the mountain, opposite Wrigley's place, which I think would be about where I saw the body fall."

"So, still feasible for Montoya to have been on the peak that night, regardless of which way he might have been pushed. If he was."

He nodded. "Still feasible."

She leaned back, then bent in half, dropping her hands to the floor to stretch her shoulders. "It looks as if the property the Wrigleys owned would be the place to start." She straightened, and her eyes met his.

He nodded agreement. "It looks that way. How early do you want to leave?"

"At least by seven, if that works for you."

"It works."

"We have a plan, then. I'll meet you downstairs at seven."

He wanted to touch her. He wanted to stay longer. He did neither.

* * *

Two things disrupted their plan. The first was a storm system that arrived around midnight, settled, and was predicted to remain strong for the next few days. The second was a quick message from Lizbeth asking him to meet her at a luxury hotel in Scottsdale for an engagement photo session after her two-day fashion show in Phoenix.

Lizbeth's note arrived soon after the one from Jade advising they needed to delay their expedition until the weather cleared. His response to Jade was simply that the timing was helpful as he had an unexpected appointment and would be out of town for a day, maybe two, but no more than that. The storm system would give him time to wrap things up.

His response to Lizbeth was just as simple. He would meet her at the hotel. He poured himself another cup of coffee, fighting the urge to add a shot of whiskey, as he made flight arrangements with a charter service. He hadn't, he realized, thought about Lizbeth *enough* since he'd been back in Albuquerque. And he wouldn't, he realized, be able to keep his thoughts *from* Jade, not just once he left, but in the lifetime after that.

As confident as he was that Jade had moved on, he knew now that he hadn't—at least not more than superficially. Maybe he never would. Lizbeth deserved better.

* * *

After a turbulent early start due to the storm system, the brief flight leveled out. The plane landed at a private airport and the limousine he'd hired was there and waiting. He allowed the driver to carry his bag from the tarmac, but not his laptop.

Once they were buckled in, the driver glanced at him in the rearview mirror. "Are you here for the golf tournament? I hear it's a spectacular group of players from all over the globe." The words were clearly from a non-golfer, but Glenn smiled and said he'd heard the same, but no, he wouldn't be golfing that weekend.

"Ah, you businessmen. Always working."

And so it went, but because the driver was pleasant and the trip short, Glenn chatted with him, revealing nothing and learning nothing in return. Still, Glenn was glad when they turned and followed a winding drive up into the foothills.

The limousine stopped at the front entrance, and the driver stepped out to open his door. "Here you go then, Sir. I hope you have a nice stay and a safe return home."

Glenn tipped him above average because someone needed to have a good day.

A young woman came from behind the check-in counter to escort him to Lizbeth, who sat in the shade of a private patio, sipping a pretty drink. Her thoughtful expression turned happy as she caught sight of him. "Oh, perfect! You made it in time for lunch. I was hoping you would. It should be out soon."

He placed his bag and laptop beside the table and leaned down to give her a hug. She glanced at his things as he took the chair across from her. "You should have had them take those up to our rooms." He hadn't because, in his heart, he didn't plan to stay. Nor, he suspected, would she want him to.

But as he looked at her, he wondered how in the hell he was going to do this. They'd never shared passionate declarations of love, but there was love between them, and they'd made a commitment to each other, and he'd had every intention of keeping that commitment. Until Jade.

"We need to talk." And those, he thought, were the ultimate words from hell.

Lizbeth eased back in her chair, and he knew she hadn't mistaken the words, his expression, or his tone for anything but the moment it was. "Famous words from every sad movie I've ever watched," she said quietly.

"I'm sorry."

"But…?"

And he told her, starting with that long ago marriage and ending with his trip to obtain Jade's signature on the divorce papers that had made that trip with him. He left out nothing except the blackmail notes and their search for a body he'd seen equally long ago.

As he talked, she sat without moving, saying nothing more than a murmured 'thank you' to the server who brought the lunch she'd ordered, along with a Whiskey Sour for him and a second John Collins for her.

When he fell silent, she said, "So you saw her, and

suddenly fell in love again." And he could see the hurt in her eyes.

"Honestly, I don't know what I feel only what I don't feel."

"...for me," she ended the sentence for him. "If you truly don't know what you feel, why not wait and see. Why end what we have, when we are so good together?"

"Because you have a beautiful heart and soul to go with the physical beauty the world sees. You deserve someone who treasures those things so much they never look further."

"Were you looking?"

"No," he said truthfully.

"I want to be mad at you, I really do, but I can't." She looked helpless. "It's sad, isn't it? If I hadn't asked you to marry me, you would never have known you were still married to this Jade. We could have lived together and been happy with that."

"Perhaps," he admitted. "Or perhaps you would eventually have realized that what we have is good, damned good, but it isn't enough for you. And it shouldn't be enough. In your heart, you know it."

"And, if you find that what this Jade and you once had is no longer there or also isn't enough? What then for you?"

"I don't know," he answered, truthfully. And that simple truth was all he had to offer.

Neither of them ate much, and when Glenn rose to leave, Lizbeth stood as well and walked into his arms, simply leaning against him for a moment before taking a step back to look up at him and whisper, "I wish you love." Her voice broke a little as she added, "This hurts ... horribly ... but I truly mean that."

"And I wish you the same, Lizbeth, and joy, forever joy.

Be safe and be happy."

Picking up his bags, he turned and walked away, feeling like the worst bastard in the history of bastards.

As he'd expected, the resort had a limousine and driver on standby for departing guests in addition to the line of taxis with drivers who knew a tip from one guest here was worth more than the fees of a dozen guests from hotels in town.

The concierge at the desk looked dismayed at his departure but brightened at his own large tip and a murmured comment from Glenn that his leaving was regrettable but unavoidable.

"Business. Of course, sir, I do understand. We hope you will visit us again very soon."

Glenn simply smiled and nodded. As beautiful and luxurious as it was, this was the last place on earth he'd care to see again. He knew the memories of his final exchange with Lizbeth here would haunt him for a long time, perhaps forever.

Chapter Twenty-eight

Jade looked out her office window at the deluge that seemed never ending. The roiling gray skies matched her mood perfectly, and now that the sun was setting somewhere behind those clouds, it was growing even darker out. For most of the day, she'd combed back through the names, the map, the notes, and the history of the area and still had come up with nothing.

The only logical conclusion was that someone had been murdered and a body discarded. Why the blackmail notes to three people, only one of whom had seen that body in a tumbling descent down the mountain? Why were the shots fired at those same three people? And while she and Glenn had a history which created a conceivable link between them, neither of them had a significant link to

Cargill nor had he any link to the mountain that she could find and certainly none in the way she and Glenn did.

And now? Now it was time, nearly time, for a fourth note to arrive. This one would have a demand for money from each of them and a place for that money to be delivered. Likely an off-shore account, she mused, something hard to trace. She'd never give in to a blackmailer's demands, nor, she suspected, would Glenn. Cargill might be willing, but he hadn't the experience of protecting himself from bullies, so the Slade Agency and the Bellamys would have his back. Still, the appearance of yielding by all three of them could give their team the edge they needed to learn the who and the why and then figure out the where sufficiently to track, find, and apprehend.

Restless, she gathered her notes and tossed them in her briefcase along with her laptop. She wasn't sure if Glenn would return for them to hit the mountain trail the next morning. If not, she'd work from her apartment.

* * *

The rain had eased slightly by the time she navigated the short distance between the office and apartment buildings. She thought about stopping for dinner at one of the local restaurants she favored, but the drizzling rain was a sufficient deterrent when she had food in her refrigerator. She wasn't happy about the slight dip in her spirits when she didn't see Glenn's truck in the parking garage, but she greeted the guard with her usual smile and reminded herself Glenn would be leaving as soon as their blackmailer was in custody. After all, he had a wedding to attend. His.

Putting thoughts of food aside, she headed straight for

her shower. The hot water eased some of her tiredness, proving her fatigue hadn't all been mental and emotional. Feeling better, she heard her phone buzz as she toweled dry and slipped on a cropped tee shirt and leggings. She hated that her pulse jumped ever so slightly when she saw Glenn's name above the message. **Dinner out or carry-out?**

Without hesitation, she answered, **carry-out anything … I'll open a bottle of wine that will go with that anything.** Dressing to go outside didn't appeal to her any more than the rain sliding sluggishly down her windowpane. At least it wasn't lashing at the glass, but still …

His response was an unexpected smile emoji. As she stared at it, she knew she was in trouble far beyond the heartache of her long-ago, eighteen-year-old self.

Wandering into her living area, she stopped at her wall of windows where the rain had resumed its attack and gazed down at the street below. She'd long since quit imagining how her life might have been and learned to love the life she lived. The cases that came their way were varied and interesting and the places it took them exciting. Sometimes maybe too exciting, as risk and danger were always a possibility.

Even so, there were moments she remembered, moments she wished for what could have been. But she kept them brief, kept them from tainting her joy in the present. The heartache of believing Glenn had simply walked away and left her had been deep, and the anger that followed even more slashing because of that grief. She'd learned how to put that anger aside.

The answers they chased now might well lead to the person or persons who'd destroyed their future together. But if they didn't, if they failed, when this case was closed and Glenn returned to the life he had created for himself, she promised herself she'd find them another way. Find out why, find out who, and make them pay.

* * *

It was, Glenn decided, fortunate that his hands were filled with carryout containers from the bar and grill that Jonah had told him made the best hamburgers around. But for that fact, he wasn't sure he could have kept his hands from following his gaze to the bare skin between her short top and the loose pants just below the curve of her waist.

They were both quiet as she helped unstack the cartons and he opened cabinet doors and drawers to find plates and flatware.

"We could eat out of the cartons," Jade commented.

"We could, but we're not."

She stopped what she was doing. "You're bossier than you were at eighteen."

He matched her look for look. "One of the hazards of creating a life from nothing." He smiled. "And you're more … everything … than you were at eighteen."

"More everything?"

"More capable. More opinionated. More determined. More beautiful." With that, he slid two wineglasses from the rack under her cabinet.

When he turned back, she was still staring at him with a look he couldn't decipher.

"White or red?" she asked.

"Your decision," he said softly. "We can talk while we eat." He wasn't unhappy that he'd caught her off-guard. There were all kinds of barriers that he'd have to breach to have what he wanted, but—for the first time in a long time—he knew exactly what that was.

He opened the wine and poured while she took water glasses and filled them from the refrigerator. Then he moved everything to the dining table while she watched with her head tilted and a faint frown on her face.

"We could eat at the bar."

"We could, but we're not," he mimicked his previous answer. He wanted to be face to face with her, wanted to watch her expressions as they talked. He wanted a lot of things, but he'd start with that.

They sorted food, then ate in silent appreciation of the taste of perfectly cooked hamburgers. He chuckled as Jade's first bite of a French-fried potato had her closing her eyes. "So good," she said appreciatively.

"Jonah said they were the best in Albuquerque."

"Jonah is right. He usually is."

"I have a question for you." She stilled at the words, and he laughed. "No hidden land mines. I promise."

Taking him at his word, she nodded. "Go ahead."

"How did the Bellamys morph from the most powerful ranchers in New Mexico to arguably being Albuquerque's most trusted ally? I didn't see a lot of politicians in the family history."

"There might have been a few," she admitted, "but they filled a need and then got out. None had any hankering for a lifetime commitment." She smiled. "And we're still among the most powerful ranchers in the state. And not everyone thinks that's a good thing."

"That doesn't explain the city's dependence on their many areas of expertise."

"You have to consider the whole of who and what we are. While Welles Enterprises, which includes the Slade Agency and Bellamy Ranch, is one of the largest employers in the state, that's only a piece of our impact. While none of the Bellamy's nor Slade's nor Welles' descendants have had long-term aspirations in politics, they were, and sometimes still are, kingmakers."

Glenn smiled. "And queenmakers?"

"In this day and time, certainly."

"Influence through money?"

"Indirectly. The corporate entities have made few direct financial contributions through the years. What influence they have on voters come more from the fact that they naturally prefer free enterprise. Voters see them contributing to things like city parks and library endowments, scholarships for students. So, those voters listen when they praise a like-minded person running for office."

"Power brokers of a sort."

"Of a sort." She smiled. "For lack of a better word."

"And you, your cousins, are a large part of what makes the family successful."

Glenn stood, carried his wine glass to the window and stared out at the rain that had slowed to a drizzle. He sensed more than heard when she followed him. "You impress me," he said.

She didn't respond, and he turned to look at her. "I wouldn't have appreciated your abilities, all you know, all you can achieve."

"Maybe you appreciate them because of all *you've* achieved." She took a deep breath. "I checked the forecast before you came up with the food. We should be good to start our search in the morning."

"Then that's what we'll do."

"Would you like a refill on that wine?"

He smiled ruefully. "No, I'll head back downstairs. We'll both need to have clear heads. The mountain isn't nearly as formidable as it once was now that there are dirt roads and hiking paths, but it's still challenging enough that we'll need to be well-rested."

He placed his glass on the counter and let himself out.

Jade watched as the door closed behind him, feeling the familiar surge of grief and anger that had chased her through the years. But that anger was no longer aimed at Glenn. They'd both been cheated, and it was possible they'd never know who or why. The realization left her with a bittersweet sadness that was almost harder to bear than the anger.

Chapter Twenty-nine

The storm from the previous night appeared to have emptied itself in the city streets, leaving nothing for the mountains in its path. Early-morning sunlight glinted on streams visible now and again.

Dust rose from the tires of an old farm truck that eased up the mountain road ahead of them. Jade felt an impatience that Glenn didn't seem to feel, or at least he didn't show it if he did. They had left before daylight, but she had been awake long before sunrise.

She felt him glancing at her now and again, and he finally asked, "What's up?"

"We're missing something." The admission galled. "*I'm* missing something."

"And today we're hunting for that something."

Looking out across the adjoining mountain peaks, she frowned. "A needle in a haystack."

She knew she sounded petulant and wouldn't have blamed him if he'd ignored her. When she turned to face him, she caught a glimpse of the smile that curved his lips, and she sighed. "I'm sorry."

He shook his head. "I understand, Jade. We're both doers, and we're at least doing something. It may not gain us anything but it just might."

"Someone could be waiting for us up here." She almost hoped they would be.

"Doubtful but possible. I have a gun and it's loaded."

"Me, too." And, at the moment, she wouldn't mind shooting a leg out from under the right someone. If only she knew who that someone was.

Because they intended to start their search at the top, near where he'd seen that body tumble, Glenn parked beside the cabin. They weren't scouring the mountain this time. Eric's topographical map narrowed their search, and, with that map to guide them, they'd be able to avoid rock climbing in their descent.

Both agreed that while the body could have dropped some distance, it seemed unlikely it would have fallen wide of their starting point. Jade shouldered her backpack, which carried water and food, as did Glenn's, and watched as he pulled a compass from his.

"I think there's a compass on my phone, if I can keep a signal."

"Mine, too, probably, but let's save those batteries."

She gave him a look, wondering what he expected to happen out here. Nothing good for sure. But, then, neither did she. Still, the most likely scenario was that they'd waste a day or two searching and come up empty-handed. At least they were making the attempt. And, she was honest with herself, the greater part of her lack of enthusiasm was knowing that when this case was solved, her last tie with Glenn would be broken. It would be easier to face that fact if he'd turned out to be an egotistical jerk or a self-centered con-artist, anything, really, but this intelligent, self-made man with a sense of humor and an inherent good-nature. He was, instead, everything she'd once believed he would be.

They started a zigzag path downward, watching for anything out of place but not really expecting to see that anything. Not after all these years. They stopped now and again, especially on a prominent point, simply to look out across the mountain and appreciate the view.

A little less than an hour later, they reached the first point of interest on Eric's map. Glenn removed his backpack and pulled out a bottle of water before dropping it to the ground. She did the same, then walked around the tumble of rocks and small boulders that almost centered a small clearing. She stared up at the outcroppings above them.

Glenn's attention was also focused on the ledge far above them.

"It's possible." She moved to look from a different angle. "A body could have been pushed from there, could have landed here," she said. "And rocks pushed after that body. Maybe rearranged a little. Maybe left where they fell."

Glenn studied those rocks and nodded.

"Could be." He pulled his phone and took a photograph of the rocks and the ledge above, then made some notes. "Or this formation could be the result of one of many natural slides over the years. Still, worth a closer look at what's underneath when we can get some equipment up here."

As they stood to go, she twisted her shoulders in a stretch, then stilled at a quick flash of light above them. Sunlight glinting on something, she told herself, a broken bottle, a scrap of metal … or a pair of binoculars trained their way. She searched the landscape above with her gaze.

"What is it?" Glenn stepped closer, turning to look in the same direction.

"I thought I saw sunlight hit glass or metal above us. I could've been mistaken."

"But you don't think so." He motioned toward the trees behind them, and she led the way. "We've kept to the open, the better to see. But we've also made it easy for someone to see us."

"You don't really think we're being followed, do you?"

"No, not really, but I'm more familiar with corporate espionage than I am guns and mountains these days."

He shrugged. "We'll go with your gut on this one and walk just inside this line of trees. Eric's map indicates a stream straight down from this clearing, not too far, with another pile of rocks to one side."

They hadn't gone far when Jade whispered. "Glenn, we *are* being followed, and I *am* sure."

"You don't have to convince me," he answered. "You have the experience here."

Before he could say more, Jade's phone vibrated, and he watched as she read the message. Her heart thudded as she relayed the information to Glenn. "It's from Jonah. Ellie and Simon have been busy, tracing property ownership, wills and deeds and entailments. Lucien Montoya *did* inherit the family property a short while before he disappeared, but it turns out the mineral rights were sold by his grandfather years before."

"Who owns them now."

She took a deep breath. "Paul Cargill. His father bought mineral rights to several properties on this mountain from owners who were struggling to survive. In Montoya's case, maybe some others, the purchases were provisionary. If the land owners were able to repay the loans plus interest prior to any mining operations beginning, they would regain those rights. Cargill started sending samples for testing about the time Montoya disappeared. Colter's on his way to Cargill's office now with questions."

Glenn was quiet a moment, then said, "Cargill may have seen something he shouldn't have or he may be in someone's way with those mineral rights. That gun you're carrying … might be a good time to pull it out." He suited his action to words as he pulled his as well.

"How good are you with a gun?" she asked. There was so much she didn't know about the boy she'd married or the man he'd become.

"Deadly with a target. Shooting toward a human…?" He shrugged.

And, that, Jade thought was where she had him beat. She smiled. "I'll have your back, cowboy."

He matched her smile for smile. "And I'll have yours, Jade."

His tone made her heart ache. She hadn't had his. She hadn't trusted he'd never leave her. She hadn't gone looking for him. Still, she reminded herself, eighteen years old, that was all she'd been then, all she'd had … just eighteen years of living and learning. It hadn't been nearly enough.

"Let's go. We'll keep to the trees and wait to hear back from Jonah."

The urge to rush was strong, but Glenn held to the same unhurried pace. If she was right and someone followed, he wouldn't want that person to know they were aware, which would have been her tactic as well. He also kept to the trees, and she agreed with that, too. A man would be a fool to try to hit a target through the thick foliage above them. All that would accomplish would be to give his presence away. Then again, maybe they were dealing with a fool. And maybe that fool had a gun.

Jade hadn't a doubt that Glenn was aware of every move she made, even though he kept his gaze busy scanning the way ahead of them and the clearing beside them and, every so often, a glance over his shoulder.

When her phone alerted her to a call, it was Colter, not Jonah. She put him on speaker with the volume down low and stepped close so Glenn could hear.

"I'm headed your way, less than an hour from the base of the mountain. Where are you?"

"Close to the old creek, not far upstream of where the families used to gather and picnic. We'll be following it down once we reach the banks."

"I went by Cargill's house, but his wife said he'd left for work, and I could catch him there." Colter's voice was grim. "His assistant said he didn't show, didn't call in, and he missed a staff meeting he'd scheduled."

"Not good," Jade agreed, "but why are you coming to us?"

"I'm thinking we need to complete this search sooner rather than later. When I get there, we'll divide and conquer."

After they broke the connection, Jade took note of Glenn's expression. "What are you thinking?"

"It's possible he had car trouble and forgot the meeting. It's also possible a fourth letter hit this morning. A demand for money and a threat of what could happen if that demand isn't met, and he went into hiding."

But both of them knew there were other possibilities, and Jade didn't much like any of them. Before they started out again, Jade tucked her pistol away. "Whoever was behind us turned away some time back. If it *was* a who, instead of a deer or mountain goat."

Glenn nodded at her words, didn't argue, but kept his gun in his hand as they started walking. They followed a stream of swift-moving water as it curved first one way then another in a downward spiral. Varicolored walls of clay, created by decades of that rushing water wearing at the earth, rose on either side of them. In some places, the banks were no more than a few feet; in others they widened into yards.

Memories, good memories, swept her. "A little farther down from here was one of my favorite places as a child." She didn't whisper but kept her voice to a murmur far below the rush of the water. "Back then, property lines didn't mean *keep out* to neighbors."

"I suspect it was more about keeping livestock in its place," Glenn agreed.

"Families would gather, dragging homemade grills and coolers of beefsteak and pork ribs and crates of pies and cookies and cupcakes. As best I recall, vegetables were optional."

"Doesn't look like much for swimming."

"No, I don't remember it ever being deep enough for swimming, but it was plenty deep for splashing and cooling off and great for chilling melons. Our entertainment was everything from corn hole competition to darts to volleyball."

She smiled at the memories. As much as the task they were here to do, she felt an urge to see what their picnic spot looked like all these years later. As they turned a bend, her breath caught at how very much the same it was with those canyon walls towering above, and a sandbar making the curve with the sweep of the water.

She stopped abruptly, trying to match memory to the landscape in front of her, and Glenn almost walked into her. "What is it?"

"Those rocks ... they shouldn't be there. I recognize the photograph Eric took but I didn't realize it was this creek, this sandbar."

She moved closer, pulling her phone from her pocket and taking pictures as she walked around it, before making a call. "Jonah, there's been a landslide on the sandbar the old folk used for cooking. Looks like it's been here a while."

"How big?"

"Big enough to hide a body."

His answer was lost to the sharp crack of a rifle, followed by the sound of earth and rock moving, the roar intensifying along with the velocity. She turned to run and heard Glenn call her name in the same instant the first sting of grit and pebbles hit her back. The ground came up to meet her as Glenn's weight covered her.

When the dust settled and the roar rumbled to silence, Glenn rolled onto his back, taking her with him. She curled against his side, giving herself this one moment out of time as his heart pounded against hers, and his hands brushed her hair from her face.

"Are you hurt?" He touched a finger to her cheek and frowned.

She supposed there would be a bruise or two but shook her head. "I'm fine, a little shaky, but fine. You?"

"I'll have an ache or two come morning."

Their eyes met, and she wondered for a moment...just for a moment. Then she heard Colter call to them. For a single heartbeat longer, Glenn held her close, then stood and pulled her to her feet.

* * *

It took several minutes for Colter and the man in front of him with a pistol pressed against his back to wind their way down to them.

Glenn would have given a hell of a lot to throw a punch into the man's face; instead, Glenn gave him a measured look and knew the other man read him well. If the court didn't deal with him, Glenn would.

"Paul Cargill." Jade said the man's name before shaking her head and turning away in disgust.

Colter looked just as disgusted. "Either of you have something I can use in place of handcuffs?"

Glenn slid his belt from the loops at his waist. "My pleasure." He wasn't particularly gentle when he pulled Cargill's arms behind him, although he was considerate enough not to break any bones or tear any ligaments.

"Thanks. Didn't want to loosen my grip on this gun to try that with mine. Damned thing might have gone off or something, and I want to see this asshole in court and behind bars."

Colter's truck was parked closer, so they headed in that direction. Together, they hoisted Cargill up into the front passenger seat, then strapped him in with the seatbelt, his arms still pulled behind his back. Glenn hoped it was as uncomfortable as it looked, but Cargill didn't say a word or even make a sound.

"Jade, can you take my pistol and hold it on him from the backseat?" Then Colter turned toward Glenn. "We'll take you back to your truck."

Glenn studied Jade's face a moment, then shook his head. "It isn't far. I've got some thinking to do and a stop to make, but I'll see you back in Albuquerque."

Chapter Thirty

Glenn went first to the cabin and walked through the tiny space as he listened to the familiar two-part call of a redwing blackbird in a nearby tree before he stepped back outside and stood looking at a view that hadn't changed much through the years. A view he'd never forgotten. The only thing missing was the teenage cowgirl with a quick smile and sparkling eyes running up to meet him.

He'd thought he'd put her behind him. Thought he'd moved on. He hadn't. He never would.

From the cabin, he went to the Bellamy-Davidson Ranch. Jade's father sat on the porch, watching the sun lowering across the horizon. Calvin stood as Glenn parked the truck. Anxious lines creased his face. "Where's Jade?"

Glenn answered his real question first. "She's fine, Sir. Headed home with Colter."

"Take a seat."

No sooner had he done that, than Jade's mother stuck her head out the door. "My girl okay?" At his nod, Missy asked her second question. "Beer or tea?"

Calvin answered for both of them. "I have a feeling we'd better have that beer, please. But I can come in and fetch them."

"You'll do no such thing. You're cooking dinner, remember?" She gave Glenn a wink, "I'll be right back." She let the door softly shut behind her.

She was as good as her word and Glenn leaned back in the chair he'd been offered. Satisfied that Jade was somewhere safe, Calvin was content to let Glenn take his time in the telling of what had happened on the mountain that day. He asked a few questions along the way, but he listened far more than he talked.

"Why do you think this Cargill got to watching you?"

"A guess would be he saw the helicopter those few days and deduced whoever had it there was interested in possibilities he'd prefer not be proven as fact."

"He had a pretty good foot in the door in Albuquerque politics, had a lot to lose with all of this."

"Without a doubt. The only thing I think might have counter-balanced that fact is that he thought he had a lot more to gain."

"So, you think maybe those mineral samples were showing traces of gold?"

"If I were a betting man."

Calvin chuckled. "Seems to me anyone in the oil business is a betting man."

With that, Glenn realized the man had cared enough to

do his homework. "I've done my share."

"You bet on my daughter."

"And she bet on me."

"What are you going to do about that?"

For a moment, Glenn said nothing, then admitted, "Hell if I know."

Calvin chuckled. "So says every wise man." He gave Glenn a look. "You seem to have a good head on your shoulders. I suspect you'll figure it out."

Glenn shared an early evening meal with Jade's parents and called Colter as he headed back to Albuquerque. Once there, he packed his things, pausing long enough to send a note with a question and an offer to Ellie that he knew she wouldn't see until morning. She, like Glenn, would make her own choices. He just wanted her to know that those choices were open to her.

* * *

Jade knew he was gone as soon as her eyes opened the next morning. She couldn't have said how she knew, she just did, so she didn't ask that question when she walked into the conference room for the Slade Agency debriefing. Her focus now, as it had always been—as she had made sure it always was—would stay fixed on the case. It surprised her a little to see Ellie at the table, seated next to Robert on one side. Jonah and Colter were on the other. She sat at the back between her uncles.

Jonah took the lead. "Some of this is conjecture, some of it is following the logic, but I believe *all* of it will be proven out when the state takes its case to court. After his father's death, Cargill found the deeds and transfers along with maps the old man had marked with places where he'd found traces of precious metals."

"Old man is an insult. Let's not let that get into the official transcript."

Jonah grunted. "Feeling a little aged, are we?"

Marcus gave his son a steely look but didn't answer.

Jonah grinned and continued, "Moving on. Cargill Junior was still an attorney and getting his start in Albuquerque politics. He needed a bankroll to boost his chances, so he began collecting and sending samples for testing without contacting the current owners. He was caught by Montoya … supposition again … who hadn't known the mineral rights were not included in his inheritance of the property. That likely led to a physical fight between Cargill and Montoya. Either Cargill knocked him out, or—just as likely—Montoya tripped and fell, striking his head on a rock or ground as hard as rock. In a panic, Cargill dragged him out of sight and came back under cover of dark to push the body over a rock outcropping. He may have had help from a couple of drifters hired to move cattle. Chances are they were paid to move on or, equally possible, their bodies, too, are out there somewhere. Montoya's body was never found—and we now know why—or will once that pile of rocks is excavated—and eventually declared deceased."

"That's a lot of supposition."

Jonah nodded, looking unconcerned. "And there's more. In his coming and going while gathering samples, we suspect Cargill saw Glenn that night. Maybe he watched him going into the cabin and worried Glenn might have seen him around where he had no business being. He got rid of him, maybe using the same drifters. After Montoya's death, Cargill gained the money he needed by selling those mineral rights back to the property owners anywhere the samples were negative for precious metals. He kept those rights anywhere the samples were positive. That last isn't supposition. Ellie did a record search and found those transactions."

He gave her a nod.

"While Ellie was busy with that, Robert had Simon looking in another direction. Cargill recently filed to run for state office. Success takes money, and lots of it."

Jade leaned forward. "So, the blackmail?"

Jonah glanced at Colter, who answered. "My theory is that he didn't expect to rake in money from either you or Glenn. He wanted to mine where the samples came back positive. One of those places is a few yards from where he buried Montoya under a rock slide like the one he tried to bury you under at the creek."

"He was afraid Montoya's remains would be found," Jade said softly.

"If and when that happened … and I'm confident it would always have been *when* rather than *if* … he'd look as innocent to you as you definitely are to him."

Reggie raised one brow. "That's a damned convoluted plot."

"I agree, but the alternative would have required him to unearth Montoya's body by himself, without equipment. It's a hell of a lot easier to cause a rockslide than to remove a pile of rock by hand. Cargill has a nice gym membership, but he's more apt to be found in the bar next door than lifting weights."

Giving a nod, Reggie looked around the room. "It feels solid. Your research, your risk-taking," he gave Jade a sharp glance at that one, then refocused on Colter. "The DA has all of this?"

"The DA and the Chief of APD."

Reggie looked at Marcus who nodded. "I'm good."

The two got to their feet and walked out together, their heads close as they talked.

Jade chuckled wryly. "I guess we passed the test. Robert, Ellie, thank you for your hard work, your smart research. It was the backbone of this case." She shifted her attention to her cousins. "I'll be in my office for the next couple of days. Thursday, I'm going back to the ranch to help with Cheney's party. Jonah, have you found Declan yet?"

"Working on it."

"Work harder."

With that, she walked out, feeling exhausted and fighting the urge to head back to the mountain.

Chapter Thirty-one

Glenn shook hands with the Realtor as they stood on his deck looking out over the ocean, while inside, a moving team was methodically and carefully packing his clothing and other personal belongings. The young man was almost beside himself at having nailed the property. "We certainly appreciate your business, sir. I'll get started on the listing as soon as I'm back in the office. Properties like this don't happen often and buyer interest will be fast and furious. And you're sure about including the furnishings?"

"I'm sure." Lizbeth had helped him pick most of the pieces. They were solid and costly and had no place where he planned to go from here.

Today, Ellie would be doing one of two things. Calling to tell him he'd lost his mind or calling to negotiate a termination on the lease of his office building. He considered not having received that call yet a good sign.

His board members were scattered across the Gulf Coast states so where they came for monthly board meetings wasn't an issue for them. His office manager and staff would accept a thirty-day severance package or make the leap with him.

He watched the Realtor leave, took one last walk along the beach, tucked his suitcases in the backseat of his truck and pulled out of his drive. His plane and pilot were ready to leave when he reached the airport, and he handed over his truck and key to the driver, who waited to make the drive to Albuquerque.

He shook hands with his pilot and stepped up into the plane. As he fastened his seatbelt, he saw the incoming message from Ellie. He read it and smiled. Starting over feels damned good. Hurry and see for yourself.

If he was making a mistake, if he was wrong about Jade, about their marriage having a chance, he'd accept that lesson and learn from it, but he'd be damned if he'd be afraid to take that chance.

* * *

Jade looked up as Robert tapped on her door. She smiled and waved him in, immediately moving to the small table so that they could sit and talk informally.

"You look chipper," she said.

"Jonah closed the deal on the purchase. The new building is ours."

"That's great news." She forced an enthusiasm she couldn't feel. This meant so much to Robert, and he deserved that from her. "Are you ready to call in the designer?"

He leaned forward. "I believe so, yes. I've walked it through a couple of times. It's a blank canvas and a spotless one. I have the layouts by floor and by room." He hesitated. "I had a thought though…"

"Go with it. I'm open to ideas."

"Well, that's a big building and it will take a while to build the team we talked about. Why don't we focus on the lab setup in the basement and my current team's offices on the first floor? I'd hate to set the next floors up, then realize we need to rearrange something."

Jade sat back in her chair and smiled. "You're going to be the best manager, Robert. That's excellent planning."

She was still smiling as he walked out, but that smile faded as she looked around her office. Taking a breath, she grabbed her purse and headed out the door. It had been a long day. Ellie was stepping onto the elevator and pressed the hold button as she walked on.

"Thanks," Jade said. "Want to go to dinner?"

"Sure." Ellie gave her a look. "So, yesterday had to be tough. Are you okay?"

For a moment, Jade thought she meant Glenn leaving, and it rattled her. She shook it off with a shrug. "Gunfire and rockslides? All in a day's work."

Ellie chuckled as they stopped at the crosswalk and waited for the pedestrian light. "Not my work day."

Dusk was settling over the city as they walked a few blocks and stepped into one of Jade's favorite restaurants, where she requested a booth near the back. The restaurant was dark and cool, and it was quiet, even though they were not the only diners.

They'd barely settled when Ellie glanced at a message on her phone. She answered it quickly, then placed it in her purse. "Sorry about that. I was waiting for that message so

I could relay some info."

"No problem," Jade said and meant it. Every Bellamy understood that the work-life balance wasn't always well-balanced.

Not until a waiter had taken their orders and they had a glass of wine in front of them did Jade ask the question she'd wondered all day. "I was surprised to see you this morning. I thought you would have headed back to Florida." With Glenn, but his name was the part she didn't, couldn't say.

"As it turns out, I'm staying in Albuquerque."

That caught Jade off-guard. "You're going to open a practice here? What about the other half of Keen & Keen?"

"Well, I'm getting rid of the half that's a cheating bastard, and I've accepted a full-time position with a private company."

Jade winced. "Damn. I'm sorry … not that you're staying, of course, but the cheating bastard part."

"Me, too." Ellie seemed pensive for a moment. "I'll admit it hit hard, and it hit without warning, but my chin is up and my shoulders are back. I'll be fine … better than fine."

"Cheers to that," Jade said softly as she lifted her wine glass. She wished she could say the same, but she could be happy for any woman who could. "And I'm glad you'll be around. I think we could be friends."

"I think we *will* be." Ellie's gaze went past her. "But for now I have to go."

Jade opened her mouth to speak, then stilled at the light touch of a hand against her neck.

Ellie got to her feet and smiled. "Hey, boss, I hope you like Seafood Arrabbiata. You owe me."

Glenn gave Ellie a small salute and slid into her place as she walked out. He looked at Jade. "Hi."

"Hi, yourself," Jade said huskily, surprised she could speak at all. "I thought you were gone."

"I was."

The knot tightened in her throat. "I guess you came back for that signature."

His gaze stayed steady on hers. "Signature?"

"On the divorce papers." She needed to get this done, needed to get away.

He shook his head. "Those went in the shredder. I don't want a divorce, Jade. If you want one, you'll have to fight me for it. I want you. I've only ever wanted you."

"Damn it," she said as the first tear fell.

Glenn chuckled as he reached his hand, palm up, across the table. Waited as she slowly put her hand in his. When his fingers closed around hers, it felt like coming home.

Author's Note

I can't say that I was ever a fan of Romeo and Juliet.
That business of dying for love does not appeal. But,
while my star-crossed lovers may have their happy-ever-
after, it won't come easily!

Thank you for taking the time to read *A Dangerous
Homecoming*. If you enjoyed it, please consider telling your
friends or posting a short review. Word of mouth is an
author's best friend and is much appreciated.
Thank you,

Susan

Also by Susan Yawn Tanner
The Bellamys of Texas historical series:
Winds Across Texas
Fire Across Texas
Storm Out of Texas

The Bellamy Legacy contemporary series:
A Dangerous Inheritance
A Dangerous Charade
A Dangerous Homecoming

New editions from Secret Staircase Books
The Scottish Highlands Romances
Highland Captive
Captive to a Dream
Exiled Heart

A Warm Southern Christmas
(a historical romance novella)

The Cat Callahan Mysteries
Callahan and the Horses of Hope
Callahan Goes Rodeo
Callahan in Action
A Callahan Christmas (short story)

Susan Yawn Tanner is a bestselling author in the romance and mystery genres. When she isn't writing, she's either tending her horses or barrel racing. Although she lives less than an hour from the Gulf of Mexico, the white sandy beaches of Mississippi can't compete with the lure of arena dirt.

Visit Susan's website to discover more about the author and her books. Sign up for her newsletter where she announces new books and exciting giveaways.
https://susanytanner.com/